A Wodehouse Miscellany

Articles and Stories

By
P.G. Wodehouse

18
EasyRead Super Large

RHYW
ReadHowYouWant Classics Library

Set in 18 pt. TiresiasLPfont

TABLE OF CONTENTS

ARTICLES

SOME ASPECTS OF GAME-CAPTAINCY

To the Game-Captain (of the football variety) the world is peopled by three classes, firstly the keen and regular player, next the partial slacker, thirdly, and lastly, the entire, abject and absolute slacker.

Of the first class, the keen and regular player, little need be said. A keen player is a gem of purest rays serene, and when to his keenness he adds regularity and punctuality, life ceases to become the mere hollow blank that it would otherwise become, and joy reigns supreme.

The absolute slacker (to take the worst at once, and have done with it) needs the pen of a Swift before adequate justice can be done to his enormities. He is a blot, an excrescence. All those moments which are not spent in avoiding games (by means of that leave which is unanimously considered the peculiar property of the French nation) he uses in concocting ingenious excuses. Armed with these, he faces with calmness the disgusting curiosity of the Game-Captain, who officiously desires to know the reason of his non-appearance on the preceding day. These excuses are of the "had-to-go-and-see-a-man-about-a-dog" type, and rarely meet with that success for which their author hopes. In the end he discovers that his chest is weak, or his heart is subject to palpitations, and he forthwith produces a document to this effect, signed by a doctor. This has the desirable result of muzzling the tyrannical Game-Captain, whose sole solace is a look of intense and withering scorn. But this is seldom fatal, and generally, we rejoice to say, ineffectual.

The next type is the partial slacker. He differs from the absolute slacker in that at rare intervals he actually turns up, changed withal into the garb of the game, and thirsting for the fray. At this point begins the time of trouble for the Game-Captain. To begin with, he is forced by stress of ignorance to ask the newcomer his name. This is, of course, an insult of the worst kind. "A being who does not know my name," argues the partial slacker, "must be something not far from a criminal lunatic." The name is, however, extracted, and the partial slacker strides to the arena. Now arises insult No.2. He is wearing his cap. A hint as to the advisability of removing this pièce de résistance not being taken, he is ordered to assume a capless state, and by these means a coolness springs up between him and the G.C. Of this the Game-Captain is made aware when the game commences. The partial slacker, scorning to insert his head in the scrum, assumes a commanding position outside and from this point criticises the Game-Captain's decisions with severity and pith. The last end of the partial slacker is generally a sad one. Stung by some pungent home-thrust, the Game-Captain is fain to try chastisement, and by these means silences the enemy's battery.

Sometimes the classes overlap. As for instance, a keen and regular player may, by some more than usually gross bit of bungling on the part of the G.-C., be moved to a fervour and eloquence worthy of Juvenal. Or, again, even the absolute slacker may for a time emulate the keen player, provided an opponent plant a shrewd kick on a tender spot. But, broadly speaking, there are only three classes.

AN UNFINISHED COLLECTION

A silence had fallen upon the smoking room. The warrior just back from the front had enquired after George Vanderpoop, and we, who knew that George's gentle spirit had, to use a metaphor after his own heart, long since been withdrawn from circulation, were feeling uncomfortable and wondering how to break the news.

Smithson is our specialist in tact, and we looked to him to be spokesman.

"George," said Smithson at last, "the late George Vanderpoop..."

"Late!" exclaimed the warrior; "is he dead?"

"As a doornail," replied Smithson sadly. "Perhaps you would care to hear the story. It is sad, but interesting. You may recollect that, when you sailed, he was starting his journalistic career. For a young writer he had done remarkably well. The *Daily Telephone* had printed two of his contributions to their correspondence column, and a bright pen picture of his, describing how Lee's Lozenges for the Liver had snatched him from almost certain death, had quite a vogue. Lee, I believe, actually commissioned him to do a series on the subject."

"Well?" said the warrior.

"Well, he was, as I say, prospering very fairly, when in an unlucky moment he began to make a collection of editorial rejection forms. He had always been a somewhat easy prey to scourges of that description. But when he had passed safely through a sharp attack of Philatelism and a rather nasty bout of Autographomania, everyone hoped and believed that he had turned the corner. The progress of his last illness was very rapid. Within a year he wanted but one specimen to make the complete set. This was the one published from the offices of the *Scrutinizer.* All the rest he had obtained with the greatest ease. I remember his telling me that a single short story of his, called 'The Vengeance of Vera Dalrymple,' had been instrumental in securing no less than thirty perfect specimens. Poor George! I was with him when he made his first attempt on the *Scrutinizer.* He had baited his hook with an essay on Evolution. He read me one or two passages from it. I stopped him at the third paragraph, and congratulated him in advance, little thinking that it was sympathy rather than congratulations that he needed. When I saw him a week afterwards he was looking haggard. I questioned him, and by slow degrees drew out the story. The article on Evolution had been printed."

"Never say die, George," I said. "Send them 'Vera Dalrymple.' No paper can take that."

"He sent it. The *Scrutinizer,* which had been running for nearly a century without publishing a line of fiction, took it and asked for more. It was as if there were an editorial conspiracy against him."

"Well?" said the man of war.

"Then," said Smithson, "George pulled himself together. He wrote a parody of 'The Minstrel Boy.' I have seen a good many parodies, but never such a parody as that. By return of post came a long envelope bearing the crest of the *Scrutinizer.* 'At last,'" he said, as he tore it open.

"George, old man," I said, "your hand."

"He looked at me a full minute. Then with a horrible, mirthless laugh he fell to the ground, and expired almost instantly. You will readily guess what killed him. The poem had been returned, *but without a rejection form!*"

THE NEW ADVERTISING

"In Denmark," said the man of ideas, coming into the smoking room, "I see that they have original ideas on the subject of advertising. According to the usually well-informed Daily Lyre, all 'bombastic' advertising is punished with a fine. The advertiser is expected to describe his wares in restrained, modest language. In case this idea should be introduced into England, I have drawn up a few specimen advertisements which, in my opinion, combine attractiveness with a shrinking modesty at which no censor could cavil."

And in spite of our protests, he began to read us his first effort, descriptive of a patent medicine.

"It runs like this," he said:

> Timson's Tonic for Distracted Deadbeats
> Has been known to cure
> We Hate to Seem to Boast, but
> Many Who have Tried It Are Still Alive

***

Take a Dose or Two in Your Spare Time
It's Not Bad Stuff

***

Read what an outside stockbroker says:

"Sir – After three months' steady absorption of your Tonic
I was no worse."

***

We do not wish to thrust ourselves forward in any way. If you prefer other medicines, by all means take them. Only we just thought we'd mention it – casually, as it were – that TIMSON'S is PRETTY GOOD.

"How's that?" inquired the man of ideas. "Attractive, I fancy, without being bombastic. Now, one about a new novel. Ready?"

MR. LUCIEN LOGROLLER'S LATEST

The Dyspepsia of the Soul
The Dyspepsia of the Soul

The Dyspepsia of the Soul

Don't buy it if you don't want to,
but just listen to a few of the criticisms.

THE DYSPEPSIA OF THE SOUL

"Rather ... rubbish."

–*Spectator*

"We advise all insomniacs to read Mr. Logroller's soporific pages."

–*Outlook*

"Rot."

–*Pelican*

THE DYSPEPSIA OF THE SOUL
Already in its first edition.

"What do you think of that?" asked the man of ideas.

We told him.

THE SECRET PLEASURES OF REGINALD

I found Reggie in the club one Saturday afternoon. He was reclining in a long chair, motionless, his eyes fixed glassily on the ceiling. He frowned a little when I spoke. "You don't seem to be doing anything," I said.

"It's not what I'm doing, it's what I am *not* doing that matters."

It sounded like an epigram, but epigrams are so little associated with Reggie that I ventured to ask what he meant.

He sighed. "Ah well," he said. "I suppose the sooner I tell you, the sooner you'll go. Do you know Bodfish?"

I shuddered. "Wilkinson Bodfish? I do."

"Have you ever spent a weekend at Bodfish's place in the country?"

I shuddered again. "I have."

"Well, I'm *not* spending the weekend at Bodfish's place in the country."

"I see you're not. But..."

"You don't understand. I do not mean that I am simply absent from Bodfish's place in the country. I mean that I am *deliberately* not spending the weekend there. When you interrupted me just now, I was not strolling down to Bodfish's garage, listening to his prattle about his new car."

I glanced around uneasily.

"Reggie, old man, you're – you're not – This hot weather..."

"I am perfectly well, and in possession of all my faculties. Now tell me. Can you imagine anything more awful than to spend a weekend with Bodfish?"

On the spur of the moment I could not.

"Can you imagine anything more delightful, then, than *not* spending a weekend with Bodfish? Well, that's what I'm doing now. Soon, when you have gone – if you have any other engagements, please don't let me keep you – I shall not go into the house and not listen to Mrs. Bodfish on the subject of young Willie Bodfish's premature intelligence."

I got his true meaning. "I see. You mean that you will be thanking your stars that you aren't with Bodfish."

"That is it, put crudely. But I go further. I don't indulge in a mere momentary self-congratulation, I do the thing thoroughly. If I were weekending at Bodfish's, I should have arrived there just half an hour ago. I therefore selected that moment for beginning not to weekend with Bodfish. I settled myself in this chair and I did not have my back slapped at the station. A few minutes later I was not whirling along the country roads, trying to balance the car with my legs and an elbow. Time passed, and I was not shaking hands with Mrs. Bodfish. I have just had the most corking half-hour, and shortly – when you have remembered an appointment – I shall go on having it. What I am really looking forward to is the happy time after dinner. I shall pass it in not playing bridge with Bodfish, Mrs. Bodfish, and a neighbor. Sunday morning is the best part of the whole weekend, though. That is when I shall most enjoy myself. Do you know a man named Pringle? Next Saturday I am not going to stay with Pringle. I forget who is not to be my host the Saturday after that. I have so many engagements of this kind that I lose track of them."

"But, Reggie, this is genius. You have hit on the greatest idea of the age. You might extend this system of yours."

"I do. Some of the jolliest evenings I have spent have been not at the theatre."

"I have often wondered what it was that made you look so fit and happy."

"Yes. These little non-visits of mine pick me up and put life into me for the coming week. I get up on Monday morning feeling like a lion. The reason I selected Bodfish this week, though I was practically engaged to a man named Stevenson who lives out in Connecticut, was that I felt rundown and needed a real rest. I shall be all right on Monday."

"And so shall I," I said, sinking into the chair beside him.

"You're not going to the country?" he asked regretfully.

"I am not. I, too, need a tonic. I shall join you at Bodfish's. I really feel a lot better already."

I closed my eyes, and relaxed, and a great peace settled upon me.

MY BATTLE WITH DRINK

I could tell my story in two words – the two words "I drank." But I was not always a drinker. This is the story of my downfall – and of my rise – for through the influence of a good woman, I have, thank Heaven, risen from the depths.

The thing stole upon me gradually, as it does upon so many young men. As a boy, I remember taking a glass of root beer, but it did not grip me then. I can recall that I even disliked the taste. I was a young man before temptation really came upon me. My downfall began when I joined the Yonkers Shorthand and Typewriting College.

It was then that I first made acquaintance with the awful power of ridicule. They were a hard-living set at college – reckless youths. They frequented movie palaces. They thought nothing of winding up an evening with a couple of egg-phosphates and a chocolate fudge. They laughed at me when I refused to join them. I was only twenty. My character was undeveloped. I could not endure their scorn. The next time I was offered a drink I accepted. They were pleased, I remember. They called me "Good old Plum!" and a good sport and other complimentary names. I was intoxicated with sudden popularity.

How vividly I can recall that day! The shining counter, the placards advertising strange mixtures with ice cream as their basis, the busy men behind the counter, the half-cynical, half-pitying eyes of the girl in the cage where you bought the soda checks. She had seen so many happy, healthy boys through that little hole in the wire netting, so many thoughtless boys all eager for their first soda, clamoring to set their foot on the primrose path that leads to destruction.

It was an apple marshmallow sundae, I recollect. I dug my spoon into it with an assumption of gaiety which I was far from feeling. The first mouthful almost nauseated me. It was like cold hair-oil. But I stuck to it. I could not break down now. I could not bear to forfeit the newly-won esteem of my comrades. They were gulping their sundaes down with the speed and enjoyment of old hands. I set my teeth, and persevered, and by degrees a strange exhilaration began to steal over me. I felt that I had burnt my boats and bridges; that I had crossed the Rubicon. I was reckless. I ordered another round. I was the life and soul of that party.

The next morning brought remorse. I did not feel well. I had pains, physical and mental. But I could not go back now. I was too weak to dispense with my popularity. I was only a boy, and on the previous evening the captain of the Checkers Club, to whom I looked up with an almost worshipping reverence, had slapped me on the back and told me that I was a corker. I felt that nothing could be excessive payment for such an honor. That night I gave a party at which orange phosphate flowed like water. It was the turning point.

I had got the habit!

I will pass briefly over the next few years. I continued to sink deeper and deeper into the slough. I knew all the drugstore clerks in New York by their first names, and they called me by mine. I no longer even had to specify the abomination I desired. I simply handed the man my ten cent check and said: "The usual, Jimmy," and he understood.

At first, considerations of health did not trouble me. I was young and strong, and my constitution quickly threw off the effects of my dissipation. Then, gradually, I began to feel worse. I was losing my grip. I found a difficulty in concentrating my attention on my work. I had dizzy spells. I became nervous and distrait. Eventually I went to a doctor. He examined me thoroughly, and shook his head.

"If I am to do you any good," he said, "you must tell me all. You must hold no secrets from me."

"Doctor," I said, covering my face with my hands, "I am a confirmed soda-fiend."

He gave me a long lecture and a longer list of instructions. I must take air and exercise and I must become a total abstainer from sundaes of all descriptions. I must avoid limeade like the plague, and if anybody offered me a Bulgarzoon I was to knock him down and shout for the nearest policeman.

I learned then for the first time what a bitterly hard thing it is for a man in a large and wicked city to keep from soda when once he has got the habit. Everything was against me. The old convivial circle began to shun me. I could not join in their revels and they began to look on me as a grouch. In the end, I fell, and in one wild orgy undid all the good of a month's abstinence. I was desperate then. I felt that nothing could save me, and I might as well give up the struggle. I drank two pin-ap-o-lades, three grapefruit-olas and an egg-zoolak, before pausing to take breath.

And then, the next day, I met May, the girl who effected my reformation. She was a clergyman's daughter who, to support her widowed mother, had accepted a non-speaking part in a musical comedy production entitled "Oh Joy! Oh Pep!" Our acquaintance ripened, and one night I asked her out to supper.

I look on that moment as the happiest of my life. I met her at the stage door, and conducted her to the nearest soda-fountain. We were inside and I was buying the checks before she realized where she was, and I shall never forget her look of mingled pain and horror.

"And I thought you were a live one!" she murmured.

It seemed that she had been looking forward to a little lobster and champagne. The idea was absolutely new to me. She quickly convinced me, however, that such was the only refreshment which she would consider, and she recoiled with unconcealed aversion from my suggestion of a Mocha Malted and an Eva Tanguay. That night I tasted wine for the first time, and my reformation began.

It was hard at first, desperately hard. Something inside me was trying to pull me back to the sundaes for which I craved, but I resisted the impulse. Always with her divinely sympathetic encouragement, I gradually acquired a taste for alcohol. And suddenly, one evening, like a flash it came upon me that I had shaken off the cursed yoke that held me down: that I never wanted to see the inside of a drugstore again. Cocktails, at first repellent, have at last become palatable to me. I drink highballs for breakfast. I am saved.

IN DEFENSE OF ASTIGMATISM

This is peculiarly an age where novelists pride themselves on the breadth of their outlook and the courage with which they refuse to ignore the realities of life; and never before have authors had such scope in the matter of the selection of heroes. In the days of the old-fashioned novel, when the hero was automatically Lord Blank or Sir Ralph Asterisk, there were, of course, certain rules that had to be observed, but today – why, you can hardly hear yourself think for the uproar of earnest young novelists proclaiming how free and unfettered they are. And yet, no writer has had the pluck to make his hero wear glasses.

In the old days, as I say, this was all very well. The hero was a young lordling, sprung from a line of ancestors who had never done anything with their eyes except wear a piercing glance before which lesser men quailed. But now novelists go into every class of society for their heroes, and surely, at least an occasional one of them must have been astigmatic. Kipps undoubtedly wore glasses; so did Bunker Bean; so did Mr. Polly, Clayhanger, Bibbs, Sheridan, and a score of others. Then why not say so?

Novelists are moving with the times in every other direction. Why not in this?

It is futile to advance the argument that glasses are unromantic. They are not. I know, because I wear them myself, and I am a singularly romantic figure, whether in my rimless, my Oxford gold-bordered, or the plain gent's spectacles which I wear in the privacy of my study.

Besides, everybody wears glasses nowadays. That is the point I wish to make. For commercial reasons, if for no others, authors ought to think seriously of this matter of goggling their heroes. It is an admitted fact that the reader of a novel likes to put himself in the hero's place – to imagine, while reading, that he is the hero. What an audience the writer of the first romance to star a spectacled hero will have. All over the country thousands of short-sighted men will polish their glasses and plunge into his pages. It is absurd to go on writing in these days for a normal-sighted public. The growing tenseness of life, with its small print, its newspapers read by artificial light, and its flickering motion pictures, is whittling down the section of the populace which has perfect sight to a mere handful.

I seem to see that romance. In fact, I think I shall write it myself. "Evadne," murmured Clarence, removing his pince-nez and polishing them tenderly... "See," cried Clarence, "how clearly every leaf of yonder tree is mirrored in the still water of the lake. I can't see myself, unfortunately, for I have left my glasses on the parlor piano, but don't worry about me: go ahead and see!" ... Clarence adjusted his tortoiseshell-rimmed spectacles with a careless gesture, and faced the assassins without a tremor. Hot stuff? Got the punch? I should say so. Do you imagine that there will be a single man in this country with the price of the book in his pocket and a pair of pince-nez on his face who will not scream and kick like an angry child if you withhold my novel from him?

And just pause for a moment to think of the serial and dramatic rights of the story. All editors wear glasses, so do all theatrical managers. My appeal will be irresistible. All I shall have to do will be to see that the check is for the right figure and to supervise the placing of the electric sign

SPECTACLES OF FATE
BY P.G. WODEHOUSE

over the doors of whichever theatre I happen to select for the production of the play.

Have you ever considered the latent possibilities for dramatic situations in short sight? You know how your glasses cloud over when you come into a warm room out of the cold? Well, imagine your hero in such a position. He has been waiting outside the murderer's den preparatory to dashing in and saving the heroine. He dashes in. "Hands up, you scoundrels," he cries. And then his glasses get all misty, and there he is, temporarily blind, with a full-size desperado backing away and measuring the distance in order to hand him one with a pickaxe.

Or would you prefer something less sensational, something more in the romantic line? Very well. Hero, on his way to the Dowager Duchess's ball, slips on a banana-peel and smashes his only pair of spectacles. He dare not fail to attend the ball, for the dear Duchess would never forgive him; so he goes in and proposes to a girl he particularly dislikes because she is dressed in pink, and the heroine told him that she was going to wear pink. But the heroine's pink dress was late in coming home from the modiste's and she had to turn up in blue. The heroine comes in just as the other girl is accepting him, and there you have a nice, live, peppy, kick-off for your tale of passion and human interest.

But I have said enough to show that the time has come when novelists, if they do not wish to be left behind in the race, must adapt themselves to modern conditions. One does not wish to threaten, but, as I say, we astigmatics are in a large minority and can, if we get together, make our presence felt. Roused by this article to a sense of the injustice of their treatment, the great army of glass-wearing citizens could very easily make novelists see reason. A boycott of non-spectacled heroes would soon achieve the necessary reform. Perhaps there will be no need to let matters go as far as that. I hope not. But, if this warning should be neglected, if we have any more of these novels about men with keen gray eyes or snapping black eyes or cheerful blue eyes – any sort of eyes,

in fact, lacking some muscular affliction, we shall know what to do.

PHOTOGRAPHERS AND ME

I look in my glass, dear reader, and what do I see? Nothing so frightfully hot, believe me. The face is slablike, the ears are large and fastened on at right-angles. Above the eyebrows comes a stagnant sea of bald forehead, stretching away into the distance with nothing to relieve it but a few wisps of lonely hair. The nose is blobby, the eyes dull, like those of a fish not in the best of health. A face, in short, taking it for all in all, which should be reserved for the gaze of my nearest and dearest who, through long habit, have got used to it and can see through to the pure white soul beneath. At any rate, a face not to be scattered about at random and come upon suddenly by nervous people and invalids.

And yet, just because I am an author, I have to keep on being photographed. It is the fault of publishers and editors, of course, really, but it is the photographer who comes in for the author's hate.

Something has got to be done about this practice of publishing authors' photographs. We have to submit to it, because editors and publishers insist. They have an extraordinary superstition that it helps an author's sales. The idea is that the public sees the photograph, pauses spell-bound for an instant, and then with a cry of ecstasy rushes off to the book-shop and buys copy after copy of the gargoyle's latest novel.

Of course, in practice, it works out just the other way. People read a review of an author's book and are told that it throbs with a passion so intense as almost to be painful, and are on the point of digging seven-and-sixpence out of their child's money-box to secure a copy, when their eyes fall on the man's photograph at the side of the review, and they find that he has a face like a rabbit and wears spectacles and a low collar. And this man is the man who is said to have laid bare the soul of a woman as with a scalpel.

Naturally their faith is shaken. They feel that a man like that cannot possibly know anything about Woman or any other subject except where to go for a vegetarian lunch, and the next moment they have put down the hair-pin and the child is seven-and-six in hand and the author his ten per cent., or whatever it is, to the bad. And all because of a photograph.

For the ordinary man, the recent introduction of high-art methods into photography has done much to diminish the unpleasantness of the operation. In the old days of crude and direct posing, there was no escape for the sitter. He had to stand up, backed by a rustic stile and a flabby canvas sheet covered with exotic trees, glaring straight into the camera. To prevent any eleventh-hour retreat, a sort of spiky thing was shoved firmly into the back of his head leaving him with the choice of being taken as he stood or having an inch of steel jabbed into his skull. Modern methods have changed all that.

There are no photographs nowadays. Only "camera portraits" and "lens impressions." The full face has been abolished. The ideal of the present-day photographer is to eliminate the sitter as far as possible and concentrate on a general cloudy effect. I have in my possession two studies of my Uncle Theodore – one taken in the early 'nineties, the other in the present year. The first shows him, evidently in pain, staring before him with a fixed expression. In his right hand he grasps a scroll. His left rests on a moss-covered wall. Two sea-gulls are flying against a stormy sky.

As a likeness, it is almost brutally exact. My uncle stands forever condemned as the wearer of a made-up tie.

The second is different in every respect. Not only has the sitter been taken in the popular modern "one-twentieth face," showing only the back of the head, the left ear and what is either a pimple or a flaw in the print, but the whole thing is plunged in the deepest shadow. It is as if my uncle had been surprised by the camera while chasing a black cat in his coal-cellar on a moonlight night. There is no question as to which of the two makes the more attractive picture. My family resemble me in that respect. The less you see of us, the better we look.

A PLEA FOR INDOOR GOLF

Indoor golf is that which is played in the home. Whether you live in a palace or a hovel, an indoor golf-course, be it only of nine holes, is well within your reach. A house offers greater facilities than an apartment, and I have found my game greatly improved since I went to live in the country. I can, perhaps, scarcely do better than give a brief description of the sporting nine-hole course which I have recently laid out in my present residence.

All authorities agree that the first hole on every links should be moderately easy, in order to give the nervous player a temporary and fictitious confidence.

At Wodehouse Manor, therefore, we drive off from the front door – in order to get the benefit of the door-mat – down an entry fairway, carpeted with rugs and without traps. The hole – a loving-cup – is just under the stairs; and a good player ought to have no difficulty in doing it in two.

The second hole, a short and simple one, takes you into the telephone booth. Trouble begins with the third, a long dog-leg hole through the kitchen into the dining-room. This hole is well trapped with table-legs, kitchen utensils, and a moving hazard in the person of Clarence the cat, who is generally wandering about the fairway. The hole is under the glass-and-china cupboard, where you are liable to be bunkered if you loft your approach-shot excessively.

The fourth and fifth holes call for no comment. They are without traps, the only danger being that you may lose a stroke through hitting the maid if she happens to be coming down the back stairs while you are taking a mashie-shot. This is a penalty under the local rule.

The sixth is the indispensable water-hole. It is short, but tricky. Teeing off from just outside the bathroom door, you have to loft the ball over the side of the bath, holing out in the little vent pipe, at the end where the water runs out.

The seventh is the longest hole on the course. Starting at the entrance of the best bedroom, a full drive takes you to the head of the stairs, whence you will need at least two more strokes to put you dead on the pin in the drawing-room.

In the drawing-room the fairway is trapped with photograph frames – with glass, complete – these serving as casual water: and anyone who can hole out on the piano in five or under is a player of class. Bogey is six, and I have known even such a capable exponent of the game as my Uncle Reginald, who is plus two on his home links on Park Avenue, to take twenty-seven at the hole. But on that occasion he had the misfortune to be bunkered in a photograph of my Aunt Clara and took no fewer than eleven strokes with his niblick to extricate himself from it.

The eighth and ninth holes are straightforward, and can be done in two and three respectively, provided you swing easily and avoid the canary's cage. Once trapped there, it is better to give up the hole without further effort. It is almost impossible to get out in less than fifty-six, and after you have taken about thirty the bird gets visibly annoyed.

THE ALARMING SPREAD OF POETRY

To the thinking man there are few things more disturbing than the realization that we are becoming a nation of minor poets. In the good old days poets were for the most part confined to garrets, which they left only for the purpose of being ejected from the offices of magazines and papers to which they attempted to sell their wares. Nobody ever thought of reading a book of poems unless accompanied by a guarantee from the publisher that the author had been dead at least a hundred years. Poetry, like wine, certain brands of cheese, and public buildings, was rightly considered to improve with age; and no connoisseur could have dreamed of filling himself with raw, indigestible verse, warm from the maker.

Today, however, editors are paying real money for poetry; publishers are making a profit on books of verse; and many a young man who, had he been born earlier, would have sustained life on a crust of bread, is now sending for the manager to find out how the restaurant dares try to sell a fellow champagne like this as genuine Pommery Brut. Naturally this is having a marked effect on the life of the community. Our children grow to adolescence with the feeling that they can become poets instead of working. Many an embryo bill clerk has been ruined by the heady knowledge that poems are paid for at the rate of a dollar a line. All over the country promising young plasterers and rising young motormen are throwing up steady jobs in order to devote themselves to the new profession. On a sunny afternoon down in Washington Square one's progress is positively impeded by the swarms of young poets brought out by the warm weather. It is a horrible sight to see those unfortunate youths, who ought to be sitting happily at desks writing

> "Dear Sir,
>
> "Your favor of the tenth inst. duly received and contents noted. In reply we beg to state..."

wandering about with their fingers in their hair and their features distorted with the agony of composition, as they try to find rhymes to "cosmic" and "symbolism."

And, as if matters were not bad enough already, along comes Mr. Edgar Lee Masters and invents *vers libre*. It is too early yet to judge the full effects of this man's horrid discovery, but there is no doubt that he has taken the lid off and unleashed forces over which none can have any control. All those decent restrictions which used to check poets have vanished, and who shall say what will be the outcome?

Until Mr. Masters came on the scene there was just one thing which, like a salient fortress in the midst of an enemy's advancing army, acted as a barrier to the youth of the country. When one's son came to one and said, "Father, I shall not be able to fulfill your dearest wish and start work in the fertilizer department. I have decided to become a poet," although one could no longer frighten him from his purpose by talking of garrets and starvation, there was still one weapon left. "What about the rhymes, Willie?" you replied, and the eager light died out of the boy's face, as he perceived the catch in what he had taken for a good thing. You pressed your advantage. "Think of having to spend your life making one line rhyme with another! Think of the bleak future, when you have used up 'moon' and 'June,' 'love' and 'dove,' 'May' and 'gay'! Think of the moment when you have ended the last line but one of your poem with 'windows' or 'warmth' and have to buckle to, trying to make the thing couple up in accordance with the rules! What then, Willie?"

Next day a new hand had signed on in the fertilizer department.

But now all that has changed. Not only are rhymes no longer necessary, but editors positively prefer them left out. If Longfellow had been writing today he would have had to revise "The Village Blacksmith" if he wanted to pull in that dollar a line. No editor would print stuff like:

> Under the spreading chestnut tree
> The village smithy stands.
> The smith a brawny man is he
> With large and sinewy hands.

If Longfellow were living in these hyphenated, free and versy days, he would find himself compelled to take his pen in hand and dictate as follows:

> In life I was the village smith,
> I worked all day

But
I retained the delicacy of my complexion
Because
I worked in the shade of the chestnut tree
Instead of in the sun
Like Nicholas Blodgett, the expressman.
I was large and strong
Because
I went in for physical culture
And deep breathing
And all those stunts.
I had the biggest biceps in Spoon River.

Who can say where this thing will end? *Vers libre* is within the reach of all. A sleeping nation has wakened to the realization that there is money to be made out of chopping its prose into bits. Something must be done shortly if the nation is to be saved from this menace. But what? It is no good shooting Edgar Lee Masters, for the mischief has been done, and even making an example of him could not undo it. Probably the only hope lies in the fact that poets never buy other poets' stuff. When once we have all become poets, the sale of verse will cease or be limited to the few copies which individual poets will buy to give to their friends.

MY LIFE AS A DRAMATIC CRITIC

I had always wanted to be a dramatic critic. A taste for sitting back and watching other people work, so essential to the make-up of this sub-species of humanity, has always been one of the leading traits in my character.

I have seldom missed a first night. No sooner has one periodical got rid of me than another has had the misfortune to engage me, with the result that I am now the foremost critic of the day, read assiduously by millions, fawned upon by managers, courted by stagehands. My lightest word can make or mar a new production. If I say a piece is bad, it dies. It may not die instantly. Generally it takes forty weeks in New York and a couple of seasons on the road to do it, but it cannot escape its fate. Sooner or later it perishes. That is the sort of man I am.

Whatever else may be charged against me, I have never deviated from the standard which I set myself at the beginning of my career. If I am called upon to review a play produced by a manager who is considering one of my own works, I do not hesitate. I praise that play.

If an actor has given me a lunch, I refuse to bite the hand that has fed me. I praise that actor's performance. I can only recall one instance of my departing from my principles. That was when the champagne was corked, and the man refused to buy me another bottle.

As is only natural, I have met many interesting people since I embarked on my career. I remember once lunching with rare Ben Jonson at the Mermaid Tavern – this would be back in Queen Elizabeth's time, when I was beginning to be known in the theatrical world – and seeing a young man with a nobby forehead and about three inches of beard doing himself well at a neighboring table at the expense of Burbage the manager.

"Ben," I asked my companion, "who is that youth?" He told me that the fellow was one Bacon, a new dramatist who had learned his technique by holding horses' heads in the Strand, and who, for some reason or other, wrote under the name of Shakespeare. "You must see his *Hamlet*," said Ben enthusiastically. "He read me the script last night. They start rehearsals at the Globe next week. It's a pippin. In the last act every blamed character in the cast who isn't already dead jumps on everyone else's neck and slays him. It's a skit, you know, on these foolish tragedies which every manager is putting on just now. Personally, I think it's the best thing since *The Prune-Hater's Daughter.*"

I was skeptical at the moment, but time proved the correctness of my old friend's judgment; and, having been present after the opening performance at a little supper given by Burbage at which sack ran like water, and anybody who wanted another malvoisie and seltzer simply had to beckon to the waiter, I was able to conscientiously praise it in the highest terms.

I still treasure the faded newspaper clipping which contains the advertisement of the play, with the legend, "Shakespeare has put one over. A scream from start to finish." – Wodehouse, in *The Weekly Bear-Baiter* (with which is incorporated *The Scurvy Knaves' Gazette*).

The lot of a dramatic critic is, in many respects, an enviable one. Lately, there has been the growing practice among critics of roasting a play on the morning after production, and then having another go at it in the Sunday edition under the title of "Second Swats" or "The Past Week in the Theatre," which has made it pretty rocky going for dramatists who thus get it twice in the same place, and experience the complex emotions of the commuter who, coming home in the dark, trips over the baby's cart and bumps his head against the hat stand.

There is also no purer pleasure than that of getting into a theatre on what the poet Milton used to call "the nod." I remember Brigham Young saying to me once with not unnatural chagrin, "You're a lucky man, Wodehouse. It doesn't cost you a nickel to go to a theatre. When I want to take in a show with the wife, I have to buy up the whole of the orchestra floor. And even then it's a tight fit."

My fellow critics and I escape this financial trouble, and it gives us a good deal of pleasure, when the male star is counting the house over the heroine's head (during their big love scene) to see him frown as he catches sight of us and hastily revise his original estimate.

THE AGONIES OF WRITING A MUSICAL COMEDY

Which Shows Why Librettists Pick at the Coverlet

The trouble about musical comedy, and the reason why a great many otherwise kindly and broadminded persons lie in wait round the corner with sudden scowls, their whole being intent on beating it with a brick the moment it shows its head, is that, from outside, it looks too easy.

You come into the crowded theatre and consider that each occupant of an orchestra chair is contributing three or four cents to the upkeep of a fellow who did nothing but dash off the stuff that keeps the numbers apart, and your blood boils. A glow of honest resentment fills you at the thought of anyone having such an absolute snap. You little know what the poor bird has suffered, and how inadequate a reward are his few yens per week for what he has been through. Musical comedy is not dashed off. It grows –

slowly and painfully, and each step in its growth either bleaches another tuft of the author's hair or removes it from the parent skull altogether.

The average musical comedy comes into being because somebody – not the public, but a manager – wants one. We will say that Mr. and Mrs. Whoosis, the eminent ballroom dancers, have decided that they require a different sphere for the exhibition of their talents. They do not demand a drama. They commission somebody to write them a musical comedy. Some poor, misguided creature is wheedled into signing a contract: and, from that moment, his troubles begin.

An inspiration gives him a pleasing and ingenious plot. Full of optimism, he starts to write it. By the time he has finished an excellent first act, he is informed that Mr. and Mrs. Whoosis propose to sing three solos and two duets in the first act and five in the second, and will he kindly build his script accordingly? This baffles the author a little. He is aware that both artistes, though extremely gifted northward as far as the ankle-bone, go all to pieces above that level, with the result that by the time you reach the zone where the brains and voice are located, there is nothing stirring whatever. And he had allowed for this in his original conception of the play, by making Mrs. Whoosis a deaf-mute and Mr. Whoosis a Trappist monk under the perpetual vow of silence. The unfolding of the plot he had left to the other characters, with a few ingenious gaps where the two stars could come on and dance.

He takes a stiff bracer, ties a vinegar-soaked handkerchief round his forehead, and sets to work to remodel his piece. He is a trifle discouraged, but he perseveres. With almost superhuman toil he contrives the only possible story which will fit the necessities of the case. He has wrapped up the script and is about to stroll round the corner to mail it, when he learns from the manager who is acting as intermediary between the parties concerned in the production that there is a slight hitch. Instead of having fifty thousand dollars deposited in the bank to back the play, it seems that the artistes merely said in their conversation that it would be awfully jolly if they *did* have that sum, or words to that effect.

By this time our author has got the thing into his system: or, rather, he has worked so hard that he feels he cannot abandon the venture now. He hunts for another manager who wants something musical, and at length finds one. The only proviso is that this manager does not need a piece built around two stars, but one suited to the needs of Jasper Cutup, the well-known comedian, whom he has under contract. The personality of Jasper is familiar to the author, so he works for a month or two and remoulds the play to fit him. With the script under his arm he staggers to the manager's office. The manager reads the script – smiles – chuckles – thoroughly enjoys it. Then a cloud passes athwart his brow. "There's only one thing the matter with this piece," he says. "You seem to have written it to star a comedian." "But you said you wanted it for Jasper Cutup," gasps the author, supporting himself against the water-cooler. "Well, yes, that is so," replies the manager. "I remember I did want a piece for him then, but he's gone and signed up with K. and Lee. What I wish you would do is to take this script and twist it to be a vehicle for Pansy Glucose."

"Pansy Glucose?" moans the author. "The ingenue?" "Yes," says the manager. "It won't take long. Just turn your Milwaukee pickle manufacturer into a debutante, and the thing is done. Get to work as soon as you can. I want this rushed."

All this is but a portion of the musical comedy author's troubles. We will assume that he eventually finds a manager who really does put the piece into rehearsal. We will even assume that he encounters none of the trials to which I have alluded. We will even go further and assume that he is commissioned to write a musical comedy without any definite stellar personality in mind, and that when he has finished it the manager will do his share by providing a suitable cast. Is he in soft? No, dear reader, he is not in soft. You have forgotten the "Gurls." Critics are inclined to reproach, deride, blame and generally hammer the author of a musical comedy because his plot is not so consecutive and unbroken as the plot of a farce or a comedy. They do not realize the conditions under which he is working. If is one of the immutable laws governing musical plays that at certain intervals during the evening the audience demand to see the chorus. They may not be aware that they so demand, but it is nevertheless a fact that, unless the chorus come on at these fixed intervals, the audience's interest sags. The raciest farce-scenes cannot hold them, nor the most tender love passages. They want the gurls, the whole gurls, and nothing but the gurls.

Thus it comes about that the author, having at last finished his first act, is roused from his dream of content by a horrid fear. He turns to the script, and discovers that his panic was well grounded. He has carelessly allowed fully twenty pages to pass without once bringing on the chorus.

This is where he begins to clutch his forehead and to grow gray at the temples. He cannot possibly shift musical number four, which is a chorus number, into the spot now occupied by musical number three, which is a duet, because three is a "situation" number, rooted to its place by the exigencies of the story. The only thing to do is to pull the act to pieces and start afresh. And when you consider that this sort of thing happens not once but a dozen times between the start of a musical comedy book and its completion, can you wonder that this branch of writing is included among the dangerous trades and that librettists always end by picking at the coverlet?

Then there is the question of cast. The author builds his hero in such a manner that he requires an actor who can sing, dance, be funny, and carry a love interest. When the time comes to cast the piece, he finds that the only possible man in sight wants fifteen hundred a week and, anyway, is signed up for the next five years with the rival syndicate. He is then faced with the alternative of revising his play to suit either:

a) Jones, who can sing and dance, but is not funny;

b) Smith, who is funny, but cannot sing and dance;

c) Brown, who is funny and can sing and dance, but who cannot carry a love-interest and, through working in revue, has developed a habit of wandering down to the footlights and chatting with the audience.

Whichever actor is given the job, it means more rewriting.

Overcome this difficulty, and another arises. Certain scenes are constructed so that A gets a laugh at the expense of B; but B is a five-hundred-a-week comedian and A is a two-hundred-a-week juvenile, and B refuses to "play straight" even for an instant for a social inferior. The original line is such that it cannot be simply switched from one to the other. The scene has to be entirely reconstructed and further laugh lines thought of. Multiply this by a hundred, and you will begin to understand why, when you see a librettist, he is generally lying on his back on the sidewalk with a crowd standing round, saying, "Give him air."

So, do not grudge the librettist his thousand a week or whatever it is. Remember what he has suffered and consider his emotions on the morning after the production when he sees lines which he invented at the cost of permanently straining his brain, attributed by the critics to the impromptu invention of the leading comedian. Of all the saddest words of tongue or pen, the saddest – to a musical comedy author – are these in the morning paper:

> "The bulk of the humor was sustained by Walter Wiffle, who gagged his way merrily through the piece."

ON THE WRITING OF LYRICS

The musical comedy lyric is an interesting survival of the days, long since departed, when poets worked. As everyone knows, the only real obstacle in the way of turning out poetry by the mile was the fact that you had to make the darned stuff rhyme.

Many lyricists rhyme as they pronounce, and their pronunciation is simply horrible. They can make "home" rhyme with "alone," and "saw" with "more," and go right off and look their innocent children in the eye without a touch of shame.

But let us not blame the erring lyricist too much. It isn't his fault that he does these things. It is the fault of the English language. Whoever invent-ed the English language must have been a prose-writer, not a versifier; for he has made meagre provision for the poets. Indeed, the word "you" is almost the only decent chance he has given them. You can do something with a word like "you." It rhymes with "sue," "eyes of blue," "woo," and all sorts of succulent things, easily fitted into the fabric of a lyric. And it has the enormous advantage that it can be repeated thrice at the end of a refrain when the composer has given you those three long notes, which is about all a composer ever thinks of. When a composer hands a lyricist a "dummy" for a song, ending thus,

> Tiddley-tum, tiddley-tum,
> Pom-pom-pom, pom-pom-pom,
> Tum, tum, tum,

the lyricist just shoves down "You, you, you" for the last line, and then sets to work to fit the rest of the words to it. I have dwelled on this, for it is noteworthy as the only bright spot in a lyricist's life, the only real cinch the poor man has.

But take the word "love."

When the board of directors, or whoever it was, was arranging the language, you would have thought that, if they had had a spark of pity in their systems, they would have tacked on to that emotion of thoughts of which the young man's fancy lightly turns in spring, some word ending in an open vowel. They must have known that lyricists would want to use whatever word they selected as a label for the above-mentioned emotion far more frequently than any other word in the language. It wasn't much to ask of them to choose a word capable of numerous rhymes. But no, they went and made it "love," causing vast misery to millions.

"Love" rhymes with "dove," "glove," "above," and "shove." It is true that poets who print their stuff instead of having it sung take a mean advantage by ringing in words like "prove" and "move"; but the lyricist is not allowed to do that. This is the wretched unfairness of the lyricist's lot. The language gets him both ways. It won't let him rhyme "love" with "move," and it won't let him rhyme "maternal" with "colonel." If he tries the first course, he is told that the rhyme, though all right for the eye, is wrong for the ear. If he tries the second course, they say that the rhyme, though more or less ninety-nine percent pure for the ear, falls short when tested by the eye. And, when he is driven back on one of the regular, guaranteed rhymes, he is taunted with triteness of phrase.

No lyricist wants to keep linking "love" with "skies above" and "turtle dove," but what can he do? You can't do a thing with "shove"; and "glove" is one of those aloof words which are not good mixers. And – mark the brutality of the thing – there is no word you can substitute for "love." It is just as if they did it on purpose.

"Home" is another example. It is the lyricist's staff of life. But all he can do is to roam across the foam, if he wants to use it. He can put in "Nome," of course, as a pinch-hitter in special crises, but very seldom; with the result that his poetic soul, straining at its bonds, goes and uses "alone," "bone," "tone," and "thrown," exciting hoots of derision.

But it is not only the paucity of rhymes that sours the lyricist's life. He is restricted in his use of material, as well. If every audience to which a musical comedy is destined to play were a metropolitan audience, all might be well; but there is the "road" to consider. And even a metropolitan audience likes its lyrics as much as possible in the language of everyday. That is one of the thousand reasons why new Gilberts do not arise. Gilbert had the advantage of being a genius, but he had the additional advantage of writing for a public which permitted him to use his full vocabulary, and even to drop into foreign languages, even Latin and a little Greek when he felt like it. (I allude to that song in "The Grand Duke.")

And yet the modern lyricist, to look on the bright side, has advantages that Gilbert never had. Gilbert never realised the possibilities of Hawaii, with its admirably named beaches, shores, and musical instruments. Hawaii – capable as it is of being rhymed with "higher" – has done much to sweeten the lot – and increase the annual income of an industrious and highly respectable but down-trodden class of the community.

THE PAST THEATRICAL SEASON

And the Six Best Performances by Unstarred Actors

What lessons do we draw from the past theatrical season?

In the first place, the success of *The Wanderer* proves that the day of the small and intimate production is over and that what the public wants is the large spectacle. In the second place, the success of *Oh, Boy!* – (I hate to refer to it, as I am one of the trio who perpetrated it; but, honestly, we're simply turning them away in droves, and Rockefeller has to touch Morgan for a bit if he wants to buy a ticket from the speculators) – proves that the day of the large spectacle is over and that what the public wants is the small and intimate production.

Then, the capacity business done by *The Thirteenth Chair* shows clearly that what the proletariat demands nowadays, is the plotty piece and that the sun of the bright dialogue comedy has set; while the capacity business done by *A Successful* Calamity shows clearly that the number of the plotty piece is up.

You will all feel better and more able to enjoy yourselves now that a trained critical mind has put you right on this subtle point.

No review of a theatrical season would be complete without a tabulated list – or even an untabulated one – of the six best performances by unstarred actors during the past season.

The present past season – that is to say, the past season which at present is the last season – has been peculiarly rich in hot efforts by all sorts of performers. My own choice would be:

1. Anna Wheaton, in *Oh, Boy!*

2. Marie Carroll, in the piece at the Princess Theatre.

3. Edna May Oliver, in Comstock and Elliott's new musical comedy.

4. Tom Powers, in the show on the south side of 39th Street.

5. Hal Forde, in the successor to *Very Good, Eddie*.

6. Stephen Maley, in *Oh, Boy!*

You would hardly credit the agony it gives me to allude, even in passing, to the above musical mélange, but one must be honest to one's public. In case there may be any who dissent from my opinion, I append a supplementary list of those entitled to honorable mention:

1. The third sheep from the O.P. side in *The Wanderer*.

2. The trick lamp in *Magic*.

3. The pink pajamas in *You're in Love*.

4. The knife in *The Thirteenth Chair*.

5. The Confused Noise Without in *The Great Divide*.

6. Jack Merritt's hair in *Oh, Boy!*

There were few discoveries among the dramatists. Of the older playwrights, Barrie produced a new one and an ancient one, but the Shakespeare boom, so strong last year, petered out. There seems no doubt that the man, in spite of a flashy start, had not the stuff. I understand that some of his things are doing fairly well on the road. Clare Kummer, whose "Dearie" I have so frequently sung in my bath, to the annoyance of all, suddenly turned right round, dropped song-writing, and ripped a couple of hot ones right over the plate. Mr. Somerset Maugham succeeded in shocking Broadway so that the sidewalks were filled with blushing ticket-speculators.

Most of the critics have done good work during this season. As for myself, I have guided the public mind in this magazine soundly and with few errors. If it were not for the fact that nearly all the plays I praised died before my review appeared, while the ones I said would not run a week are still packing them in, I could look back to a flawless season.

As you can see, I have had a very pleasant theatrical season. The weather was uniformly fine on the nights when I went to the theatre. I was particularly fortunate in having neighbors at most of the plays who were not afflicted with coughs or a desire to explain the plot to their wives. I have shaken hands with A.L. Erlanger and been nodded to on the street by Lee Shubert. I have broadened my mind by travel on the road with a theatrical company, with the result that, if you want to get me out of New York, you will have to use dynamite.

Take it for all in all, a most satisfactory season, full of pregnant possibilities – and all that sort of thing.

POEMS

DAMON AND PYTHIAS

A Romance

Since Earth was first created,
Since Time began to fly,
No friends were e'er so mated,
So firm as JONES and I.
Since primal Man was fashioned
To people ice and stones,
No pair, I ween, had ever been
Such chums as I and JONES.

In fair and foulest weather,
Beginning when but boys,
We faced our woes together,
We shared each other's joys.
Together, sad or merry,
We acted hand in glove,
Until – 'twas careless, very–
I chanced to fall in love.

The lady's points to touch on,
Her name was JULIA WHITE,
Her lineage high, her scutcheon
Untarnished; manners, bright;

Complexion, soft and creamy;
Her hair, of golden hue;
Her eyes, in aspect, dreamy,
In colour, greyish blue.

For her I sighed, I panted;
I saw her in my dreams;
I vowed, protested, ranted;
I sent her chocolate creams.
Until methought one morning
I seemed to hear a voice,
A still, small voice of warning.
"Does JONES approve your choice?"

To JONES of my affection
I spoke that very night.
If he had no objection,
I said I'd wed Miss WHITE.
I asked him for his blessing,
But, turning rather blue,
He said: "It's most distressing,
But *I* adore her, too."

"Then, JONES," I answered, sobbing,
"My wooing's at an end,
I couldn't think of robbing
My best, my only friend.

The notion makes me furious–
I'd much prefer to die."
"Perhaps you'll think it curious,"
Said JONES, "but so should I."

Nor he nor I would falter
In our resolve one jot.
I bade him seek the altar,
He vowed that he would not.
"She's yours, old fellow. Make her
As happy as you can."
"Not so," said I, "you take her–
You are the lucky man."

At length – the situation
Had lasted now a year–
I had an inspiration,
Which seemed to make things clear.
"Supposing," I suggested,
"We ask Miss WHITE to choose?
I should be interested
To hear her private views.

"Perhaps she has a preference–
I own it sounds absurd–
But I submit, with deference,
That she might well be heard.

In clear, commercial diction
The case in point we'll state,
Disclose the cause of friction,
And leave the rest to Fate."

We did, and on the morrow
The postman brought us news.
Miss WHITE expressed her sorrow
At having to refuse.
Of all her many reasons
This seemed to me the pith:
Six months before (or rather more)
She'd married Mr. SMITH.

THE HAUNTED TRAM

Ghosts of The Towers, The Grange, The Court,
Ghosts of the Castle Keep.
Ghosts of the finicking, "high-life" sort
Are growing a trifle cheap.
But here is a spook of another stamp,
No thin, theatrical sham,
But a spectre who fears not dirt nor damp:
He rides on a London tram.

By the curious glance of a mortal eye
He is not seen. He's heard.
His steps go a-creeping, creeping by,
He speaks but a single word.
You may hear his feet: you may hear them plain,
For – it's odd in a ghost – they crunch.
You may hear the whirr of his rattling chain,
And the ting of his ringing punch.

The gathering shadows of night fall fast;
The lamps in the street are lit;
To the roof have the eerie footsteps passed,
Where the outside passengers sit.
To the passenger's side has the spectre paced;

For a moment he halts, they say,
Then a ring from the punch at the unseen waist,
And the footsteps pass away.

That is the tale of the haunted car;
And if on that car you ride
You won't, believe me, have journeyed far
Ere the spectre seeks your side.
Ay, all unseen by your seat he'll stand,
And (unless it's a wig) your hair
Will rise at the touch of his icy hand,
And the sound of his whispered "Fare!"

At the end of the trip, when you're getting down
(And you'll probably simply fly!)
Just give the conductor half-a-crown,
Ask who is the ghost and why.
And the man will explain with bated breath
(And point you a moral) thus:
"'E's a pore young bloke wot wos crushed to death
By people as fought
As they didn't ought
For seats on a crowded bus."

STORIES

WHEN PAPA SWORE IN HINDUSTANI

"Sylvia!"

"Yes, papa."

"That infernal dog of yours..."

"Oh, papa!"

"Yes, that infernal dog of yours has been at my carnations again!"

Colonel Reynolds, V.C., glared sternly across the table at Miss Sylvia Reynolds, and Miss Sylvia Reynolds looked in a deprecatory manner back at Colonel Reynolds, V.C.; while the dog in question – a foppish pug – happening to meet the colonel's eye in transit, crawled unostentatiously under the sideboard, and began to wrestle with a bad conscience.

"Oh, naughty Tommy!" said Miss Reynolds mildly, in the direction of the sideboard.

"Yes, my dear," assented the colonel; "and if you could convey to him the information that if he does it once more – yes, just once more! – I shall shoot him on the spot you would be doing him a kindness." And the colonel bit a large crescent out of his toast, with all the energy and conviction of a man who has thoroughly made up his mind. "At six o'clock this morning," continued he, in a voice of gentle melancholy, "I happened to look out of my bedroom window, and saw him. He had then destroyed two of my best plants, and was commencing on a third, with every appearance of self-satisfaction. I threw two large brushes and a boot at him."

"Oh, papa! They didn't hit him?"

"No, my dear, they did not. The brushes missed him by several yards, and the boot smashed a fourth carnation. However, I was so fortunate as to attract his attention, and he left off."

"I can't think what makes him do it. I suppose it's bones. He's got bones buried all over the garden."

"Well, if he does it again, you'll find that there will be a few more bones buried in the garden!"

said the colonel grimly; and he subsided into his paper.

Sylvia loved the dog partly for its own sake, but principally for that of the giver, one Reginald Dallas, whom it had struck at an early period of their acquaintance that he and Miss Sylvia Reynolds were made for one another. On communicating this discovery to Sylvia herself he had found that her views upon the subject were identical with his own; and all would have gone well had it not been for a melancholy accident.

One day while out shooting with the colonel, with whom he was doing his best to ingratiate himself, with a view to obtaining his consent to the match, he had allowed his sporting instincts to carry him away to such a degree that, in sporting parlance, he wiped his eye badly. Now, the colonel prided himself with justice on his powers as a shot; but on this particular day he had a touch of liver, which resulted in his shooting over the birds, and under the birds, and on each side of the birds, but very rarely at the birds. Dallas being in especially good form, it was found, when the bag came to be counted, that, while he had shot seventy brace, the colonel had only managed to secure five and a half!

His bad marksmanship destroyed the last remnant of his temper. He swore for half an hour in Hindustani, and for another half-hour in English. After that he felt better. And when, at the end of dinner, Sylvia came to him with the absurd request that she might marry Mr. Reginald Dallas he did not have a fit, but merely signified in fairly moderate terms his entire and absolute refusal to think of such a thing.

This had happened a month before, and the pug, which had changed hands in the earlier days of the friendship, still remained, at the imminent risk of its life, to soothe Sylvia and madden her father.

It was generally felt that the way to find favour in the eyes of Sylvia – which were a charming blue, and well worth finding favour in – was to show an intelligent and affectionate interest in her dog. This was so up to a certain point; but no farther, for the mournful recollection of Mr. Dallas prevented her from meeting their advances in quite the spirit they could have wished.

However, they persevered, and scarcely a week went by in which Thomas was not rescued from an artfully arranged horrible fate by somebody.

But all their energy was in reality wasted, for Sylvia remembered her faithful Reggie, who corresponded vigorously every day, and refused to be put off with worthless imitations. The lovesick swains, however, could not be expected to know of this, and the rescuing of Tommy proceeded briskly, now one, now another, playing the rôle of hero.

The very day after the conversation above recorded had taken place a terrible tragedy occurred.

The colonel, returning from a poor day's shooting, observed through the mist that was beginning to rise a small form busily engaged in excavating in the precious carnation-bed. Slipping in a cartridge, he fired; and the skill which had deserted him during the day came back to him. There was a yelp; then silence. And Sylvia, rushing out from the house, found the luckless Thomas breathing his last on a heap of uprooted carnations.

The news was not long in spreading. The cook told the postman, and the postman thoughtfully handed it on to the servants at the rest of the houses on his round. By noon it was public property; and in the afternoon, at various times from two to five, nineteen young men were struck, quite independently of one another, with a brilliant idea.

The results of this idea were apparent on the following day.

"Is this all?" asked the colonel of the servant, as she brought in a couple of letters at breakfast-time.

"There's a hamper for Miss Sylvia, sir."

"A hamper, is there? Well, bring it in."

"If you please, sir, there's several of them."

"What? Several? How many are there?"

"Nineteen, sir," said Mary, restraining with some difficulty an inclination to giggle.

"Eh? What? Nineteen? Nonsense! Where are they?"

"We've put them in the coachhouse for the present, sir. And if you please, sir, cook says she thinks there's something alive in them."

"Something alive?"

"Yes, sir. And John says he thinks it's dogs, sir!"

The colonel uttered a sound that was almost a bark, and, followed by Sylvia, rushed to the coachhouse. There, sure enough, as far as the eye could reach, were the hampers; and, as they looked, a sound proceeded from one of them that was unmistakably the plaintive note of a dog that has been shut up, and is getting tired of it.

Instantly the other eighteen hampers joined in, until the whole coachhouse rang with the noise.

The colonel subsided against a wall, and began to express himself softly in Hindustani.

"Poor dears!" said Sylvia. "How stuffy they must be feeling!"

She ran to the house, and returned with a basin of water.

"Poor dears!" she said again. "You'll soon have something to drink."

She knelt down by the nearest hamper, and cut the cord that fastened it. A pug jumped out like a jack-in-the-box, and rushed to the water. Sylvia continued her work of mercy, and by the time the colonel had recovered sufficiently to be able to express his views in English, eighteen more pugs had joined their companion.

"Get out, you brute!" shouted the colonel, as a dog insinuated itself between his legs. "Sylvia, put them back again this minute! You had no business to let them out. Put them back!"

"But I can't, papa. I can't catch them."

She looked helplessly from him to the seething mass of dogs, and back again.

"Where's my gun?" began the colonel.

"Papa, don't! You couldn't be so cruel! They aren't doing any harm, poor things!"

"If I knew who sent them..."

"Perhaps there's something to show. Yes; here's a visiting-card in this hamper."

"Whose is it?" bellowed the colonel through the din.

"J. D'Arcy Henderson, The Firs,"

read Sylvia, at the top of her voice.

"Young blackguard!" bawled the colonel.

"I expect there's one in each of the hampers. Yes; here's another. W.K. Ross, The Elms."

The colonel came across, and began to examine the hampers with his own hand. Each hamper contained a visiting-card, and each card bore the name of a neighbour. The colonel returned to the breakfast-room, and laid the nineteen cards out in a row on the table.

"H'm!" he said, at last. "Mr. Reginald Dallas does not seem to be represented."

Sylvia said nothing.

"No; he seems not to be represented. I did not give him credit for so much sense." Then he dropped the subject, and breakfast proceeded in silence.

A young gentleman met the colonel on his walk that morning.

"Morning, colonel!" said he.

"Good-morning!" said the colonel grimly.

"Er – colonel, I – er – suppose Miss Reynolds got that dog all right?"

"To which dog do you refer?"

"It was a pug, you know. It ought to have arrived by this time."

"Yes. I am inclined to think it has. Had it any special characteristics?"

"No, I don't think so. Just an ordinary pug."

"Well, young man, if you will go to my coachhouse, you will find nineteen ordinary pugs; and if you would kindly select your beast, and shoot it, I should be much obliged."

"Nineteen?" said the other, in astonishment. "Why, are you setting up as a dog-fancier in your old age, colonel?"

This was too much for the colonel. He exploded.

"Old age! Confound your impudence! Dog-fancier! No, sir! I have not become a dog-fancier in what you are pleased to call my old age! But while there is no law to prevent a lot of dashed young puppies like yourself, sir – like yourself – sending your confounded pug-dogs to my daughter, who ought to have known better than to have let them out of their dashed hampers, I have no defence.

"Dog-fancier! Gad! Unless those dogs are removed by this time tomorrow, sir, they will go straight to the Battersea Home, where I devoutly trust they will poison them. Here are the cards of the other gentlemen who were kind enough to think that I might wish to set up for a dog-fancier in my old age. Perhaps you will kindly return them to their owners, and tell them what I have just said." And he strode off, leaving the young man in a species of trance.

"Sylvia!" said the colonel, on arriving home.

"Yes, papa."

"Do you still want to marry that Dallas fellow? Now, for Heaven's sake, don't start crying! Goodness knows I've been worried enough this morning without that. Please answer a plain question in a fairly sane manner. Do you, or do you not?"

"Of course I do, papa."

"Then you may. He's the furthest from being a fool of any of the young puppies who live about here, and he knows one end of a gun from the other. I'll write to him now."

> "Dear Dallas" (wrote the colonel) – "I find, on consideration, that you are the only sensible person in the neighbourhood. I hope you will come to lunch today. And if you still want to marry my daughter, you may."

To which Dallas replied by return of messenger:

"Thanks for both invitations. I will."

An hour later he arrived in person, and the course of true love pulled itself together, and began to run smooth again.

TOM, DICK, AND HARRY

This story will interest and amuse all cricketers, and while from the male point of view it may serve as a good illustration of the fickleness of woman and the impossibility of forecasting what course she will take, the fair sex will find in it an equally shining proof of the colossal vanity of man.

"It's like this."

Tom Ellison sat down on the bed, and paused.

"Whack it out," said Dick Henley encouragingly.

"We're all friends here, and the password's 'Portland.' What's the matter?"

"I hate talking to a man when he's shaving. I don't want to have you cutting your head off."

"Don't worry about me. This is a safety razor. And, anyhow, what's the excitement? Going to make my flesh creep?"

Tom Ellison kicked uncomfortably at the chair he was trying to balance on one leg.

"It's so hard to explain."

"Have a dash at it."

"Well, look here, Dick, we've always been pals. What?"

"Of course we have."

"We went to the Empire last Boatrace night together..."

"And got chucked out simultaneously."

"In fact, we've always been pals. What?"

"Of course we have."

"Then, whenever there was a rag on, and a bonner in the quad, you always knew you could help yourself to my chairs."

"You had the run of mine."

"We've shared each other's baccy."

"And whisky."

"In short, we've always been pals. What?"

"Of course we have."

"Then," said Tom Ellison, "what are you trying to cut me out for?"

"Cut you out?"

"You know what I mean. What do you think I came here for? To play cricket? Rot! I'd much rather have gone on tour with the Authentics. I came here to propose to Dolly Burn."

Dick Henley frowned.

"I wish you'd speak of her as Miss Burn," he said austerely.

"There you are, you see," said Tom with sombre triumph; "you oughtn't to have noticed a thing like that. It oughtn't to matter to you what I call her. I always think of her as Dolly."

"You've no right to."

"I shall have soon."

"I'll bet you won't."

"How much?"

"Ten to one in anything."

"Done," said Tom. "I mean," he added hastily, "don't be a fool. There are some things one can't bet on. As you ought to have known," he said primly.

"Now, look here," said Dick, "this thing has got to be settled. You say I'm trying to cut you out. I like that! We may fairly describe that as rich. As if my love were the same sort of passing fancy that yours is. You know you fall in love, as you call it, with every girl you meet."

"I don't."

"Very well. If the subject is painful we won't discuss it. Still, how about that girl you used to rave about last summer? Ethel Something?"

Tom blushed.

"A mere platonic friendship. We both collected autographs. And, if it comes to that, how about Dora Thingummy? You had enough to say about her last winter."

Dick reddened.

"We were on good terms. Nothing more. She always sliced with her brassy. So did I. It formed a sort of bond."

There was a pause.

"After all," resumed Dick, "I don't see the point of all this. Why rake up the past? You aren't writing my life."

"You started raking."

"Well, to drop that, what do you propose to do about this? You're a good chap, Tom, when you aren't making an ass of yourself; but I'm hanged if I'm going to have you interfering between me and Dolly."

"Miss Burn."

Another pause.

"Look here," said Dick. "Cards on the table. I've loved her since last Commem."

"So have I."

"We went up the Char together in a Canader. Alone."

"She also did the trip with me. No chaperone."

"Twice with me."

"Same here."

"She gave me a couple of dances at the Oriel ball."

"So she did me. She said my dancing was so much better than the average young man's."

"She told me I must have had a great deal of practice at waltzing."

"In the matter of photographs," said Tom, "she gave me one."

"Me, too."

"Do you mean 'also' or 'a brace'?" inquired Tom anxiously.

"Also," confessed Dick with reluctance.

"Signed?"

"Rather!"

A third pause.

"I tell you what it is," said Tom; "we must agree on something, or we shall both get left. All we're doing now is to confuse the poor girl. She evidently likes us both the same. What I mean is, we're both so alike that she can't possibly make a choice unless one of us chucks it. You don't feel like chucking it, Dick. What?"

"You needn't be more of an idiot than you can help."

"I only asked. So we are evidently both determined to stick to it. We shall have to toss, then, to settle which is to back out and give the other man a show."

"Toss!" shouted Dick. "For Dolly! Never!"

"But we must do something. You won't back out like a sensible man. We must settle it somehow."

"It's all right," said Dick. "I've got it. We both seem to have come here and let ourselves in for this rotten little village match, on a wicket which will probably be all holes and hillocks, simply for Dolly's sake. So it's only right that we should let the match decide this thing for us. It won't be so cold-blooded as tossing. See?"

"You mean...?"

"Whichever of us makes the bigger score today wins. The loser has to keep absolutely off the grass. Not so much as a look or a remark about the weather. Then, of course, after the winner has had his innings, if he hasn't brought the thing off, and she has chucked him, the loser can have a look in. But not a moment before. Understand?"

"All right."

"It'll give an interest to a rotten match," said Dick.

Tom rose to a point of order.

"There's one objection. You, being a stodgy sort of bat, and having a habit of sitting on the splice, always get put in first. I'm a hitter, so they generally shove me in about fourth wicket. In this sort of match the man who goes in fourth wicket is likely to be not out half a dozen at the end of the innings. Nobody stays in more than three balls. Whereas you, going in first, will have time for a decent knock before the rot starts. Follow?"

"I don't want to take any advantage of you," said Dick condescendingly. "I shan't need it. We'll see Drew after breakfast and get him to put us both in first."

The Rev. Henry Drew, cricketing curate, was the captain of the side.

Consulted on the matter after breakfast, the Rev. Henry looked grave. He was taking this match very seriously, and held decided views on the subject of managing his team.

"The point is, my dear Ellison," he said, "that I want the bowling broken a bit before you go in. Then your free, aggressive style would have a better chance. I was thinking of putting you in fourth wicket. Would not that suit you?"

"I thought so. Tell him, Dick."

"Look here, Drew," said Dick; "you'll regard what I'm going to say as said under seal of the confessional and that sort of thing, won't you?"

"I shall, of course, respect any confidence you impart to me, my dear Henley. What is this dreadful secret?"

Dick explained.

"So you see," he concluded, "it's absolutely necessary that we should start fair."

The Rev. Henry looked as disturbed as if he had suddenly detected symptoms of Pelagianism in a member of his Sunday-school class.

"Is such a contest quite...? Is it not a little – um?" he said.

"Not at all," said Dick, hastening to justify himself and friend. "We must settle the thing somehow, and neither of us will back out. If we didn't do this we should have to toss."

"Heaven forbid!" said the curate, shocked.

"Well, is it a deal? Will you put us in first?"

"Very well."

"Thanks," said Tom.

"Good of you," said Dick.

"Don't mention it," said Harry.

***

There are two sorts of country cricket. There is the variety you get at a country-house, where the wicket is prepared with a care as meticulous as that in fashion on any county ground; where red marl and such-like aids to smoothness have been injected into the turf all through the winter; and where the out-fielding is good and the boundaries spacious. And there is the village match, where cows are apt to stroll on to the pitch before the innings and cover-point stands up to his neck in a furze-bush.

The game which was to decide the fate of Tom and Dick belonged to the latter variety. A pitch had been mown in the middle of a meadow (kindly lent by Farmer Rollitt on condition that he should be allowed to umpire, and his eldest son Ted put on to bowl first). The team consisted of certain horny-handed sons of toil, with terrific golf-shots in the direction of square-leg, and the enemy's ranks were composed of the same material. Tom and Dick, in ordinary circumstances, would have gone in to bat in such a match with a feeling of lofty disdain, as befitting experts from the civilised world, come to teach the rustic mind what was what.

But on the present occasion the thought of all that depended on their bats induced a state of nerves which would have done credit to a test match.

"Would you mind taking first b-b-ball, old man?" said Tom.

"All r-right," said Dick. He had been on the point of making the request himself, but it would not do to let Tom see that he was nervous.

He took guard from Farmer Rollitt, and settled himself into position to face the first delivery.

Whether it is due to the pure air of the country or to daily manual toil is not known, but the fact remains that bowlers in village matches, whatever their other shortcomings, seldom fall short in the matter of speed. The present trundler, having swung his arm round like a flail, bounded to the crease and sent down a ball which hummed in the air. It pitched halfway between the wickets in a slight hollow caused by the foot of a cow and shot.

Dick reached blindly forward, and the next moment his off-stump was out of the ground.

A howl of approval went up from the supporters of the enemy, lying under the trees.

Tom sat down, limp with joy. Dick out for a duck! What incredible good fortune! He began to frame in his mind epigrammatic sentences for use in the scene which would so shortly take place between Miss Dolly Burn and himself. The next man came in and played flukily but successfully through the rest of the over. "Just a single," said Tom to himself as he faced the bowler at the other end. "Just one solitary single. Miss Burn – may I call you Dolly? Do you remember that moonlight night? On the Char? In my Canadian canoe? We two?"

"'S THAT?" shrieked bowler and wicket-keeper as one man.

Tom looked blankly at them. He had not gone within a mile and a half of the ball, he was certain. And yet – there was the umpire with his hand raised, as if he were the Pope bestowing a blessing.

He walked quickly back to the trees, flung off his pads, and began to smoke furiously.

"Well?" said a voice.

Dick was standing before him, grinning like a gargoyle.

"Of all the absolutely delirious decisions..." began Tom.

"Oh, yes," said Dick rudely, "I know all about that. Why, I could hear the click from where I was sitting. The point is, what's to be done now? We shall have to settle it on the second innings."

"If there is one."

"Oh, there'll be a second innings all right. There's another man out. On a wicket like this we shall all be out in an hour, and we'll have the other side out in another hour, and then we'll start again on this business. I shall play a big game next innings. It was only that infernal ball shooting that did me."

"And I," said Tom; "if the umpire has got over his fit of delirium tremens, or been removed to Colney Hatch, shall almost certainly make a century."

It was four o'clock by the time Tom and Dick went to the wickets for the second time. Their side had been headed by their opponents by a dozen on the first innings – 68 to 56.

A splendid spirit of confidence animated the two batsmen. The umpire who had effected Tom's downfall in the first innings had since received a hard drive in the small of the back as he turned coyly away to avoid the ball, and was now being massaged by strong men in the tap-room of the village inn. It was the sort of occurrence, said Tom, which proved once and for all the existence of an all-seeing, benevolent Providence.

As for Dick, he had smoothed out a few of the more important mountain-ranges which marred the smoothness of the wicket, and was feeling that all was right with the world.

The pair started well. The demon bowler of the enemy, having been fêted considerably under the trees by enthusiastic admirers during the innings of his side, was a little incoherent in his deliveries. Four full-pitches did he send down to Dick in his first over, and Dick had placed 16 to his credit before Tom, who had had to look on anxiously, had opened his account. Dick was a slow scorer as a rule, but he knew a full-pitch to leg when he saw one.

From his place at the other crease Tom could see Miss Burn and her mother sitting under the trees, watching the game.

The sight nerved him. By the time he had played through his first over he had reduced Dick's lead by half. An oyster would have hit out in such circumstances, and Tom was always an aggressive batsman. By the end of the third over the scores were level. Each had made 20.

Enthusiasm ran high amongst the spectators, or such of them as were natives of the village. Such a stand for the first wicket had not been seen in all the matches ever played in the neighbourhood. When Tom, with a nice straight drive (which should have been a 4, but was stopped by a cow and turned into a single), brought up the century, small boys burst buttons and octogenarians wept like babes.

The bowling was collared. The demon had long since retired grumbling to the deep field. Weird trundlers, with actions like nothing else on earth, had been tried, had fired their ringing shot, and passed. One individual had gone on with lobs, to the acute delight of everybody except the fields-men who had to retrieve the balls and the above-mentioned cow. And still Tom and Dick stayed in and smote, while in the west the sun slowly sank.

The Rev. Henry looked anxious. It was magnificent, but it must not be overdone. A little more and they would not have time to get the foe out for the second time. In which case the latter would win on the first innings. And this thought was as gall to him.

He walked out and addressed the rival captain.

"I think," said he, "we will close our innings."

Tom and Dick made two bee-lines for the scorer and waited palpitatingly for the verdict.

"What's my score?" panted Tom.

"Fifty-fower, sur."

"And mine?" gasped Dick.

"Fifty-fower, too, sur."

***

"You see, my dear fellows," said the Rev. Henry when they had finished – and his voice was like unto oil that is poured into a wound – "we had to win this match, and if you had gone on batting we should not have had time to get them out. As it is, we shall have to hurry."

"But, hang it..." said Tom.

"But, look here..." said Dick.

"Yes?"

"What on earth are we to do?" said Tom.

"We're in precisely the same hole as we were before," said Dick.

"We don't know how to manage it."

"We're absolutely bunkered."

"Our competition, you see."

"About Miss Burn, don't you know."

"Which is to propose first?"

"We can't settle it."

The Rev. Henry smiled a faint, saintly smile and raised a protesting hand.

"My advice," he said, "is that both of you should refrain from proposing."

"What?" said Dick.

"*Wha-at?*" said Tom.

"You see," purred the Rev. Henry, "you are both very young fellows. Probably you do not know your own minds. You take these things too seri..."

"Now, look here," said Tom.

"None of that rot," said Dick.

"I shall propose tonight."

"I shall propose this evening."

"I shouldn't," said the Rev. Henry. "The fact is..."

"Well?"

"Well?"

"I didn't tell you before, for fear it should put you off your game; but Miss Burn is engaged already, and has been for three days."

The two rivals started.

"Engaged!" cried Tom.

"Whom to?" hissed Dick.

"Me," murmured Harry.

JEEVES TAKES CHARGE

Now, touching this business of old Jeeves – my man, you know – how do we stand? Lots of people think I'm much too dependent on him. My Aunt Agatha, in fact, has even gone so far as to call him my keeper. Well, what I say is: Why not? The man's a genius. From the collar upward he stands alone. I gave up trying to run my own affairs within a week of his coming to me. That was about half a dozen years ago, directly after the rather rummy business of Florence Craye, my Uncle Willoughby's book, and Edwin, the Boy Scout.

The thing really began when I got back to Easeby, my uncle's place in Shropshire. I was spending a week or so there, as I generally did in the summer; and I had had to break my visit to come back to London to get a new valet. I had found Meadowes, the fellow I had taken to Easeby with me, sneaking my silk socks, a thing no bloke of spirit could stick at any price. It transpiring, moreover, that he had looted a lot of other things here and there about the place, I was reluctantly compelled to hand the misguided blighter the mitten and go to London to ask the registry office to dig up another specimen for my approval. They sent me Jeeves.

I shall always remember the morning he came. It so happened that the night before I had been present at a rather cheery little supper, and I was feeling pretty rocky. On top of this I was trying to read a book Florence Craye had given me. She had been one of the house-party at Easeby, and two or three days before I left we had got engaged. I was due back at the end of the week, and I knew she would expect me to have finished the book by then. You see, she was particularly keen on boosting me up a bit nearer her own plane of intellect. She was a girl with a wonderful profile, but steeped to the gills in serious purpose. I can't give you a better idea of the way things stood than by telling you that the book she'd given me to read was called "Types of Ethical Theory," and that when I opened it at random I struck a page beginning:–

> *The postulate or common understanding involved in speech is certainly co-extensive, in the obligation it carries, with the social*

> *organism of which language is the instrument, and the ends of which it is an effort to subserve.*

All perfectly true, no doubt; but not the sort of thing to spring on a lad with a morning head.

I was doing my best to skim through this bright little volume when the bell rang. I crawled off the sofa and opened the door. A kind of darkish sort of respectful Johnnie stood without.

"I was sent by the agency, sir," he said. "I was given to understand that you required a valet."

I'd have preferred an undertaker; but I told him to stagger in, and he floated noiselessly through the doorway like a healing zephyr. That impressed me from the start. Meadowes had had flat feet and used to clump. This fellow didn't seem to have any feet at all. He just streamed in. He had a grave, sympathetic face, as if he, too, knew what it was to sup with the lads.

"Excuse me, sir," he said gently.

Then he seemed to flicker, and wasn't there any longer. I heard him moving about in the kitchen, and presently he came back with a glass on a tray.

"If you would drink this, sir," he said, with a kind of bedside manner, rather like the royal doctor shooting the bracer into the sick prince. "It is a little preparation of my own invention. It is the Worcester Sauce that gives it its colour. The raw egg makes it nutritious. The red pepper gives it its bite. Gentlemen have told me they have found it extremely invigorating after a late evening."

I would have clutched at anything that looked like a life-line that morning. I swallowed the stuff. For a moment I felt as if somebody had touched off a bomb inside the old bean and was strolling down my throat with a lighted torch, and then everything seemed suddenly to get all right. The sun shone in through the window; birds twittered in the tree-tops; and, generally speaking, hope dawned once more.

"You're engaged!" I said, as soon as I could say anything.

I perceived clearly that this cove was one of the world's wonders, the sort no home should be without.

"Thank you, sir. My name is Jeeves."

"You can start in at once?"

"Immediately, sir."

"Because I'm due down at Easeby, in Shropshire, the day after tomorrow."

"Very good, sir." He looked past me at the mantelpiece. "That is an excellent likeness of Lady Florence Craye, sir. It is two years since I saw her ladyship. I was at one time in Lord Worplesdon's employment. I tendered my resignation because I could not see eye to eye with his lordship in his desire to dine in dress trousers, a flannel shirt, and a shooting coat."

He couldn't tell me anything I didn't know about the old boy's eccentricity. This Lord Worplesdon was Florence's father. He was the old buster who, a few years later, came down to breakfast one morning, lifted the first cover he saw, said

"Eggs! Eggs! Eggs! Damn all eggs!" in an overwrought sort of voice, and instantly legged it for France, never to return to the bosom of his family. This, mind you, being a bit of luck for the bosom of the family, for old Worplesdon had the worst temper in the county.

I had known the family ever since I was a kid, and from boyhood up this old boy had put the fear of death into me. Time, the great healer, could never remove from my memory the occasion when he found me – then a stripling of fifteen – smoking one of his special cigars in the stables. He got after me with a hunting-crop just at the moment when I was beginning to realise that what I wanted most on earth was solitude and repose, and chased me more than a mile across difficult country. If there was a flaw, so to speak, in the pure joy of being engaged to Florence, it was the fact that she rather took after her father, and one was never certain when she might erupt. She had a wonderful profile, though.

"Lady Florence and I are engaged, Jeeves," I said.

"Indeed, sir?"

You know, there was a kind of rummy something about his manner. Perfectly all right and all that, but not what you'd call chirpy. It somehow gave me the impression that he wasn't keen on Florence. Well, of course, it wasn't my business. I supposed that while he had been valeting old Worplesdon she must have trodden on his toes in some way. Florence was a dear girl, and, seen sideways, most awfully good-looking; but if she had a fault it was a tendency to be a bit imperious with the domestic staff.

At this point in the proceedings there was another ring at the front door. Jeeves shimmered out and came back with a telegram. I opened it. It ran:

> *Return immediately. Extremely urgent. Catch first train. Florence.*

"Rum!" I said.

"Sir?"

"Oh, nothing!"

It shows how little I knew Jeeves in those days that I didn't go a bit deeper into the matter with him. Nowadays I would never dream of reading a rummy communication without asking him what he thought of it. And this one was devilish odd. What I mean is, Florence knew I was going back to Easeby the day after tomorrow, anyway; so why the hurry call? Something must have happened, of course; but I couldn't see what on earth it could be.

"Jeeves," I said, "we shall be going down to Easeby this afternoon. Can you manage it?"

"Certainly, sir."

"You can get your packing done and all that?"

"Without any difficulty, sir. Which suit will you wear for the journey?"

"This one."

I had on a rather sprightly young check that morning, to which I was a good deal attached; I fancied it, in fact, more than a little. It was perhaps rather sudden till you got used to it, but, nevertheless, an extremely sound effort, which many lads at the club and elsewhere had admired unrestrainedly.

"Very good, sir."

Again there was that kind of rummy something in his manner. It was the way he said it, don't you know. He didn't like the suit. I pulled myself together to assert myself. Something seemed to tell me that, unless I was jolly careful and nipped this lad in the bud, he would be starting to boss me. He had the aspect of a distinctly resolute blighter.

Well, I wasn't going to have any of that sort of thing, by Jove! I'd seen so many cases of fellows who had become perfect slaves to their valets. I remember poor old Aubrey Fothergill telling me – with absolute tears in his eyes, poor chap! – one night at the club, that he had been compelled to give up a favourite pair of brown shoes simply because Meekyn, his man, disapproved of them. You have to keep these fellows in their place, don't you know. You have to work the good old iron-hand-in-the-velvet-glove wheeze. If you give them a what's-its-name, they take a thingummy.

"Don't you like this suit, Jeeves?" I said coldly.

"Oh, yes, sir."

"Well, what don't you like about it?"

"It is a very nice suit, sir."

"Well, what's wrong with it? Out with it, dash it!"

"If I might make the suggestion, sir, a simple brown or blue, with a hint of some quiet twill..."

"What absolute rot!"

"Very good, sir."

"Perfectly blithering, my dear man!"

"As you say, sir."

I felt as if I had stepped on the place where the last stair ought to have been, but wasn't. I felt defiant, if you know what I mean, and there didn't seem anything to defy.

"All right, then," I said.

"Yes, sir."

And then he went away to collect his kit, while I started in again on "Types of Ethical Theory" and took a stab at a chapter headed "Idiopsychological Ethics."

***

Most of the way down in the train that afternoon, I was wondering what could be up at the other end. I simply couldn't see what could have happened. Easeby wasn't one of those country houses you read about in the society novels, where young girls are lured on to play baccarat and then skinned to the bone of their jewellery, and so on. The house-party I had left had consisted entirely of law-abiding birds like myself.

Besides, my uncle wouldn't have let anything of that kind go on in his house. He was a rather stiff, precise sort of old boy, who liked a quiet life. He was just finishing a history of the family or something, which he had been working on for the last year, and didn't stir much from the library. He was rather a good instance of what they say about its being a good scheme for a fellow to sow his wild oats. I'd been told that in his youth Uncle Willoughby had been a bit of a rounder. You would never have thought it to look at him now.

When I got to the house, Oakshott, the butler, told me that Florence was in her room, watching her maid pack. Apparently there was a dance on at a house about twenty miles away that night, and she was motoring over with some of the Easeby lot and would be away some nights. Oakshott said she had told him to tell her the moment I arrived; so I trickled into the smoking-room and waited, and presently in she came. A glance showed me that she was perturbed, and even peeved. Her eyes had a goggly look, and altogether she appeared considerably pipped. "Darling!" I said, and attempted the good old embrace; but she sidestepped like a bantam weight.

"Don't!"

"What's the matter?"

"Everything's the matter! Bertie, you remember asking me, when you left, to make myself pleasant to your uncle?"

"Yes."

The idea being, of course, that as at that time I was more or less dependent on Uncle Willoughby I couldn't very well marry without his approval. And though I knew he wouldn't have any objection to Florence, having known her father since they were at Oxford together, I hadn't wanted to take any chances; so I had told her to make an effort to fascinate the old boy.

"You told me it would please him particularly if I asked him to read me some of his history of the family."

"Wasn't he pleased?"

"He was delighted. He finished writing the thing yesterday afternoon, and read me nearly all of it last night. I have never had such a shock in my life. The book is an outrage. It is impossible. It is horrible!"

"But, dash it, the family weren't so bad as all that."

"It is not a history of the family at all. Your uncle has written his reminiscences! He calls them 'Recollections of a Long Life'!"

I began to understand. As I say, Uncle Willoughby had been somewhat on the tabasco side as a young man, and it began to look as if he might have turned out something pretty fruity if he had started recollecting his long life.

"If half of what he has written is true," said Florence, "your uncle's youth must have been perfectly appalling. The moment we began to read he plunged straight into a most scandalous story of how he and my father were thrown out of a music-hall in 1887!"

"Why?"

"I decline to tell you why."

It must have been something pretty bad. It took a lot to make them chuck people out of music-halls in 1887.

"Your uncle specifically states that father had drunk a quart and a half of champagne before beginning the evening," she went on. "The book is full of stories like that. There is a dreadful one about Lord Emsworth."

"Lord Emsworth? Not the one we know? Not the one at Blandings?"

A most respectable old Johnnie, don't you know. Doesn't do a thing nowadays but dig in the garden with a spud.

"The very same. That is what makes the book so unspeakable. It is full of stories about people one knows who are the essence of propriety today, but who seem to have behaved, when they were in London in the 'eighties, in a manner that would not have been tolerated in the fo'c'sle of a whaler. Your uncle seems to remember everything disgraceful that happened to anybody when he was in his early twenties. There is a story about Sir Stanley Gervase-Gervase at Rosherville Gardens which is ghastly in its perfection of detail. It seems that Sir Stanley – but I can't tell you!"

"Have a dash!"

"No!"

"Oh, well, I shouldn't worry. No publisher will print the book if it's as bad as all that."

"On the contrary, your uncle told me that all negotiations are settled with Riggs and Ballinger, and he's sending off the manuscript tomorrow for immediate publication. They make a special thing of that sort of book. They published Lady Carnaby's 'Memories of Eighty Interesting Years.'"

"I read 'em!"

"Well, then, when I tell you that Lady Carnaby's Memories are simply not to be compared with your uncle's Recollections, you will understand my state of mind. And father appears in nearly every story in the book! I am horrified at the things he did when he was a young man!"

"What's to be done?"

"The manuscript must be intercepted before it reaches Riggs and Ballinger, and destroyed!"

I sat up.

This sounded rather sporting.

"How are you going to do it?" I enquired.

"How can I do it? Didn't I tell you the parcel goes off tomorrow? I am going to the Murgatroyds' dance tonight and shall not be back till Monday. You must do it. That is why I telegraphed to you."

"What!"

She gave me a look.

"Do you mean to say you refuse to help me, Bertie?"

"No; but – I say!"

"It's quite simple."

"But even if I – What I mean is – Of course, anything I can do – but – if you know what I mean..."

"You say you want to marry me, Bertie?"

"Yes, of course; but still..."

For a moment she looked exactly like her old father.

"I will never marry you if those Recollections are published."

"But, Florence, old thing!"

"I mean it. You may look on it as a test, Bertie. If you have the resource and courage to carry this thing through, I will take it as evidence that you are not the vapid and shiftless person most people think you. If you fail, I shall know that your Aunt Agatha was right when she called you a spineless invertebrate and advised me strongly not to marry you. It will be perfectly simple for you to intercept the manuscript, Bertie. It only requires a little resolution."

"But suppose Uncle Willoughby catches me at it? He'd cut me off with a bob."

"If you care more for your uncle's money than for me..."

"No, no! Rather not!"

"Very well, then. The parcel containing the manuscript will, of course, be placed on the hall table tomorrow for Oakshott to take to the village with the letters. All you have to do is to take it away and destroy it. Then your uncle will think it has been lost in the post."

It sounded thin to me.

"Hasn't he got a copy of it?"

"No; it has not been typed. He is sending the manuscript just as he wrote it."

"But he could write it over again."

"As if he would have the energy!"

"But..."

"If you are going to do nothing but make absurd objections, Bertie..."

"I was only pointing things out."

"Well, don't! Once and for all, will you do me this quite simple act of kindness?"

The way she put it gave me an idea.

"Why not get Edwin to do it? Keep it in the family, kind of, don't you know. Besides, it would be a boon to the kid."

A jolly bright idea it seemed to me. Edwin was her young brother, who was spending his holidays at Easeby. He was a ferret-faced kid, whom I had disliked since birth. As a matter of fact, talking of Recollections and Memories, it was young blighted Edwin who, nine years before, had led his father to where I was smoking his cigar and caused all of the unpleasantness. He was fourteen now and had just joined the Boy Scouts. He was one of those thorough kids, and took his responsibilities pretty seriously. He was always in a sort of fever because he was dropping behind schedule with his daily acts of kindness. However hard he tried, he'd fall behind; and then you would find him prowling about the house, setting such a clip to try and catch up with himself that Easeby was rapidly becoming a perfect hell for man and beast.

The idea didn't seem to strike Florence.

"I shall do nothing of the kind, Bertie. I wonder you can't appreciate the compliment I am paying you – trusting you like this."

"Oh, I see that all right, but what I mean is, Edwin would do it so much better than I would. These Boy Scouts are up to all sorts of dodges. They spoor, don't you know, and take cover and creep about, and what not."

"Bertie, will you or will you not do this perfectly trivial thing for me? If not, say so now, and let us end this farce of pretending that you care a snap of the fingers for me."

"Dear old soul, I love you devotedly!"

"Then will you or will you not..."

"Oh, all right," I said. "All right! All right! All right!"

And then I tottered forth to think it over. I met Jeeves in the passage just outside.

"I beg your pardon, sir. I was endeavouring to find you."

"What's the matter?"

"I felt that I should tell you, sir, that somebody has been putting black polish on our brown walking shoes."

"What! Who? Why?"

"I could not say, sir."

"Can anything be done with them?"

"Nothing, sir."

"Damn!"

"Very good, sir."

***

I've often wondered since then how these murderer fellows manage to keep in shape while they're contemplating their next effort. I had a much simpler sort of job on hand, and the thought of it rattled me to such an extent in the night watches that I was a perfect wreck next day. Dark circles under the eyes – I give you my word! I had to call on Jeeves to rally round with one of those life-savers of his.

From breakfast on I felt like a bag-snatcher at a railway station. I had to hang about waiting for the parcel to be put on the hall table, and it wasn't put. Uncle Willoughby was a fixture in the library, adding the finishing touches to the great work, I supposed, and the more I thought the thing over the less I liked it. The chances against my pulling it off seemed about three to two, and the thought of what would happen if I didn't gave me cold shivers down the spine. Uncle Willoughby was a pretty mild sort of old boy, as a rule, but I've known him to cut up rough, and, by Jove, he was scheduled to extend himself if he caught me trying to get away with his life work.

It wasn't till nearly four that he toddled out of the library with the parcel under his arm, put it on the table, and toddled off again. I was hiding a bit to the south-east at the moment, behind a suit of armour. I bounded out and legged it for the table. Then I nipped upstairs to hide the swag. I charged in like a mustang and nearly stubbed my toe on young blighted Edwin, the Boy Scout. He was standing at the chest of drawers, confound him, messing about with my ties.

"Hallo!" he said.

"What are you doing here?"

"I'm tidying your room. It's my last Saturday's act of kindness."

"Last Saturday's?"

"I'm five days behind. I was six till last night, but I polished your shoes."

"Was it you..."

"Yes. Did you see them? I just happened to think of it. I was in here, looking round. Mr. Berkeley had this room while you were away. He left this morning. I thought perhaps he might have left something in it that I could have sent on. I've often done acts of kindness that way."

"You must be a comfort to one and all!"

It became more and more apparent to me that this infernal kid must somehow be turned out eftsoons or right speedily. I had hidden the parcel behind my back, and I didn't think he had seen it; but I wanted to get at that chest of drawers quick, before anyone else came along.

"I shouldn't bother about tidying the room," I said.

"I like tidying it. It's not a bit of trouble – really."

"But it's quite tidy now."

"Not so tidy as I shall make it."

This was getting perfectly rotten. I didn't want to murder the kid, and yet there didn't seem any other way of shifting him. I pressed down the mental accelerator. The old lemon throbbed fiercely. I got an idea.

"There's something much kinder than that which you could do," I said. "You see that box of cigars? Take it down to the smoking-room and snip off the ends for me. That would save me no end of trouble. Stagger along, laddie."

He seemed a bit doubtful; but he staggered. I shoved the parcel into a drawer, locked it, trousered the key, and felt better. I might be a chump, but, dash it, I could out-general a mere kid with a face like a ferret. I went downstairs again. Just as I was passing the smoking-room door, out curveted Edwin. It seemed to me that if he wanted to do a real act of kindness he would commit suicide.

"I'm snipping them," he said.

"Snip on! Snip on!"

"Do you like them snipped much, or only a bit?"

"Medium."

"All right. I'll be getting on, then."

"I should."

And we parted.

Fellows who know all about that sort of thing – detectives, and so on – will tell you that the most difficult thing in the world is to get rid of the body. I remember, as a kid, having to learn by heart a poem about a bird by the name of Eugene Aram, who had the deuce of a job in this respect. All I can recall of the actual poetry is the bit that goes:

Tum-tum, tum-tum, tum-tumty-tum,
I slew him, tum-tum-tum!

But I recollect that the poor blighter spent much of his valuable time dumping the corpse into ponds and burying it, and what not, only to have it pop out at him again. It was about an hour after I had shoved the parcel into the drawer when I realised that I had let myself in for just the same sort of thing.

Florence had talked in an airy sort of way about destroying the manuscript; but when one came down to it, how the deuce can a chap destroy a great chunky mass of paper in somebody else's house in the middle of summer? I couldn't ask to have a fire in my bedroom, with the thermometer in the eighties. And if I didn't burn the thing, how else could I get rid of it? Fellows on the battle-field eat dispatches to keep them from falling into the hands of the enemy, but it would have taken me a year to eat Uncle Willoughby's Recollections.

I'm bound to say the problem absolutely baffled me. The only thing seemed to be to leave the parcel in the drawer and hope for the best.

I don't know whether you have ever experienced it, but it's a dashed unpleasant thing having a crime on one's conscience. Towards the end of the day the mere sight of the drawer began to depress me. I found myself getting all on edge; and once when Uncle Willoughby trickled silently into the smoking-room when I was alone there and spoke to me before I knew he was there, I broke the record for the sitting high jump.

I was wondering all the time when Uncle Willoughby would sit up and take notice. I didn't think he would have time to suspect that anything had gone wrong till Saturday morning, when he would be expecting, of course, to get the acknowledgment of the manuscript from the publishers. But early on Friday evening he came out of the library as I was passing and asked me to step in. He was looking considerably rattled.

"Bertie," he said – he always spoke in a precise sort of pompous kind of way – "an exceedingly disturbing thing has happened. As you know, I dispatched the manuscript of my book to Messrs. Riggs and Ballinger, the publishers, yesterday afternoon. It should have reached them by the first post this morning. Why I should have been uneasy I cannot say, but my mind was not altogether at rest respecting the safety of the parcel. I therefore telephoned to Messrs. Riggs and Ballinger a few moments back to make enquiries. To my consternation they informed me that they were not yet in receipt of my manuscript."

"Very rum!"

"I recollect distinctly placing it myself on the hall table in good time to be taken to the village. But here is a sinister thing. I have spoken to Oakshott, who took the rest of the letters to the post office, and he cannot recall seeing it there. He is, indeed, unswerving in his assertions that when he went to the hall to collect the letters there was no parcel among them."

"Sounds funny!"

"Bertie, shall I tell you what I suspect?"

"What's that?"

"The suspicion will no doubt sound to you incredible, but it alone seems to fit the facts as we know them. I incline to the belief that the parcel has been stolen."

"Oh, I say! Surely not!"

"Wait! Hear me out. Though I have said nothing to you before, or to anyone else, concerning the matter, the fact remains that during the past few weeks a number of objects – some valuable, others not – have disappeared in this house. The conclusion to which one is irresistibly impelled is that we have a kleptomaniac in our midst. It is a peculiarity of kleptomania, as you are no doubt aware, that the subject is unable to differentiate between the intrinsic values of objects. He will purloin an old coat as readily as a diamond ring, or a tobacco pipe costing but a few shillings with the same eagerness as a purse of gold. The fact that this manuscript of mine could be of no possible value to any outside person convinces me that..."

"But, uncle, one moment; I know all about those things that were stolen. It was Meadowes, my man, who pinched them. I caught him snaffling my silk socks. Right in the act, by Jove!"

He was tremendously impressed.

"You amaze me, Bertie! Send for the man at once and question him."

"But he isn't here. You see, directly I found that he was a sock-sneaker I gave him the boot. That's why I went to London – to get a new man."

"Then, if the man Meadowes is no longer in the house it could not be he who purloined my manuscript. The whole thing is inexplicable."

After which we brooded for a bit. Uncle Willoughby pottered about the room, registering baffledness, while I sat sucking at a cigarette, feeling rather like a chappie I'd once read about in a book, who murdered another cove and hid the body under the dining-room table, and then had to be the life and soul of a dinner party, with it there all the time. My guilty secret oppressed me to such an extent that after a while I couldn't stick it any longer. I lit another cigarette and started for a stroll in the grounds, by way of cooling off.

It was one of those still evenings you get in the summer, when you can hear a snail clear its throat a mile away. The sun was sinking over the hills and the gnats were fooling about all over the place, and everything smelled rather topping – what with the falling dew and so on – and I was just beginning to feel a little soothed by the peace of it all when suddenly I heard my name spoken.

"It's about Bertie."

It was the loathsome voice of young blighted Edwin! For a moment I couldn't locate it. Then I realised that it came from the library. My stroll had taken me within a few yards of the open window.

I had often wondered how those Johnnies in books did it – I mean the fellows with whom it was the work of a moment to do about a dozen things that ought to have taken them about ten minutes. But, as a matter of fact, it was the work of a moment with me to chuck away my cigarette, swear a bit, leap about ten yards, dive into a bush that stood near the library window, and stand there with my ears flapping. I was as certain as I've ever been of anything that all sorts of rotten things were in the offing.

"About Bertie?" I heard Uncle Willoughby say.

"About Bertie and your parcel. I heard you talking to him just now. I believe he's got it."

When I tell you that just as I heard these frightful words a fairly substantial beetle of sorts dropped from the bush down the back of my neck, and I couldn't even stir to squash the same, you will understand that I felt pretty rotten. Everything seemed against me.

"What do you mean, boy? I was discussing the disappearance of my manuscript with Bertie only a moment back, and he professed himself as perplexed by the mystery as myself."

"Well, I was in his room yesterday afternoon, doing him an act of kindness, and he came in with a parcel. I could see it, though he tried to keep it behind his back. And then he asked me to go to the smoking-room and snip some cigars for him;

and about two minutes afterwards he came down – and he wasn't carrying anything. So it must be in his room."

I understand they deliberately teach these dashed Boy Scouts to cultivate their powers of observation and deduction and what not. Devilish thoughtless and inconsiderate of them, I call it. Look at the trouble it causes.

"It sounds incredible," said Uncle Willoughby, thereby bucking me up a trifle.

"Shall I go and look in his room?" asked young blighted Edwin. "I'm sure the parcel's there."

"But what could be his motive for perpetrating this extraordinary theft?"

"Perhaps he's a – what you said just now."

"A kleptomaniac? Impossible!"

"It might have been Bertie who took all those things from the very start," suggested the little brute hopefully. "He may be like Raffles."

"Raffles?"

"He's a chap in a book who went about pinching things."

"I cannot believe that Bertie would – ah – go about pinching things."

"Well, I'm sure he's got the parcel. I'll tell you what you might do. You might say that Mr. Berkeley wired that he had left something here. He had Bertie's room, you know. You might say you wanted to look for it."

"That would be possible. I..."

I didn't wait to hear any more. Things were getting too hot. I sneaked softly out of my bush and raced for the front door. I sprinted up to my room and made for the drawer where I had put the parcel. And then I found I hadn't the key. It wasn't for the deuce of a time that I recollected I had shifted it to my evening trousers the night before and must have forgotten to take it out again.

Where the dickens were my evening things? I had looked all over the place before I remembered that

Jeeves must have taken them away to brush. To leap at the bell and ring it was, with me, the work of a moment. I had just rung it when there was a footstep outside, and in came Uncle Willoughby.

"Oh, Bertie," he said, without a blush, "I have – ah – received a telegram from Berkeley, who occupied this room in your absence, asking me to forward him his – er – his cigarette-case, which, it would appear, he inadvertently omitted to take with him when he left the house. I cannot find it downstairs; and it has, therefore, occurred to me that he may have left it in this room. I will – er – just take a look around."

It was one of the most disgusting spectacles I've ever seen – this white-haired old man, who should have been thinking of the hereafter, standing there lying like an actor.

"I haven't seen it anywhere," I said.

"Nevertheless, I will search. I must – ah – spare no effort."

"I should have seen it if it had been here – what?"

"It may have escaped your notice. It is – er – possibly in one of the drawers."

He began to nose about. He pulled out drawer after drawer, pottering around like an old bloodhound, and babbling from time to time about Berkeley and his cigarette-case in a way that struck me as perfectly ghastly. I just stood there, losing weight every moment.

Then he came to the drawer where the parcel was.

"This appears to be locked," he said, rattling the handle.

"Yes; I shouldn't bother about that one. It – it's – er – locked, and all that sort of thing."

"You have not the key?"

A soft, respectful voice spoke behind me.

"I fancy, sir, that this must be the key you require. It was in the pocket of your evening trousers."

It was Jeeves. He had shimmered in, carrying my evening things, and was standing there holding out the key. I could have massacred the man.

"Thank you," said my uncle.

"Not at all, sir."

The next moment Uncle Willoughby had opened the drawer. I shut my eyes.

"No," said Uncle Willoughby, "there is nothing here. The drawer is empty. Thank you, Bertie. I hope I have not disturbed you. I fancy – er – Berkeley must have taken his case with him after all."

When he had gone I shut the door carefully. Then I turned to Jeeves. The man was putting my evening things out on a chair.

"Er – Jeeves!"

"Sir?"

"Oh, nothing."

It was deuced difficult to know how to begin.

"Er – Jeeves!"

"Sir?"

"Did you – Was there – Have you by chance..."

"I removed the parcel this morning, sir."

"Oh – ah – why?"

"I considered it more prudent, sir."

I mused for a while.

"Of course, I suppose all this seems tolerably rummy to you, Jeeves?"

"Not at all, sir. I chanced to overhear you and Lady Florence speaking of the matter the other evening, sir."

"Did you, by Jove?"

"Yes, sir."

"Well – er – Jeeves, I think that, on the whole, if you were to – as it were – freeze on to that parcel until we get back to London..."

"Exactly, sir."

"And then we might – er – so to speak – chuck it away somewhere – what?"

"Precisely, sir."

"I'll leave it in your hands."

"Entirely, sir."

"You know, Jeeves, you're by way of being rather a topper."

"I endeavour to give satisfaction, sir."

"One in a million, by Jove!"

"It is very kind of you to say so, sir."

"Well, that's about all, then, I think."

"Very good, sir."

Florence came back on Monday. I didn't see her till we were all having tea in the hall. It wasn't till the crowd had cleared away a bit that we got a chance of having a word together.

"Well, Bertie?" she said.

"It's all right."

"You have destroyed the manuscript?"

"Not exactly; but..."

"What do you mean?"

"I mean I haven't absolutely..."

"Bertie, your manner is furtive!"

"It's all right. It's this way..."

And I was just going to explain how things stood when out of the library came leaping Uncle Willoughby looking as braced as a two-year-old. The old boy was a changed man.

"A most remarkable thing, Bertie! I have just been speaking with Mr. Riggs on the telephone, and he tells me he received my manuscript by the first post this morning. I cannot imagine what can have caused the delay. Our postal facilities are extremely inadequate in the rural districts. I shall write to headquarters about it. It is insufferable if valuable parcels are to be delayed in this fashion."

I happened to be looking at Florence's profile at the moment, and at this juncture she swung round and gave me a look that went right through me like a knife. Uncle Willoughby meandered back to the library, and there was a silence that you could have dug bits out of with a spoon.

"I can't understand it," I said at last. "I can't understand it, by Jove!"

"I can. I can understand it perfectly, Bertie. Your heart failed you. Rather than risk offending your uncle you..."

"No, no! Absolutely!"

"You preferred to lose me rather than risk losing the money. Perhaps you did not think I meant what I said. I meant every word. Our engagement is ended."

"But – I say!"

"Not another word!"

"But, Florence, old thing!"

"I do not wish to hear any more. I see now that your Aunt Agatha was perfectly right. I consider that I have had a very lucky escape. There was a time when I thought that, with patience, you might be moulded into something worth while. I see now that you are impossible!"

And she popped off, leaving me to pick up the pieces. When I had collected the debris to some extent I went to my room and rang for Jeeves. He came in looking as if nothing had happened or was ever going to happen. He was the calmest thing in captivity.

"Jeeves!" I yelled. "Jeeves, that parcel has arrived in London!"

"Yes, sir?"

"Did you send it?"

"Yes, sir. I acted for the best, sir. I think that both you and Lady Florence overestimated the danger of people being offended at being mentioned in Sir Willoughby's Recollections. It has been my experience, sir, that the normal person enjoys seeing his or her name in print, irrespective of what is said about them. I have an aunt, sir, who a few years ago was a martyr to swollen limbs. She tried Walkinshaw's Supreme Ointment and obtained considerable relief – so much so that she sent them an unsolicited testimonial. Her pride at seeing her photograph in the daily papers in connection with descriptions of her lower limbs before taking, which were nothing less than revolting, was so intense that it led me to believe that publicity, of whatever sort, is what nearly everybody desires. Moreover, if you have ever studied psychology, sir, you will know that respectable old gentlemen are by no means averse to having it advertised that they were extremely wild in their youth. I have an uncle..."

I cursed his aunts and his uncles and him and all the rest of the family.

"Do you know that Lady Florence has broken off her engagement with me?"

"Indeed, sir?"

Not a bit of sympathy! I might have been telling him it was a fine day.

"You're sacked!"

"Very good, sir."

He coughed gently.

"As I am no longer in your employment, sir, I can speak freely without appearing to take a liberty. In my opinion you and Lady Florence were quite unsuitably matched. Her ladyship is of a highly determined and arbitrary temperament, quite opposed to your own. I was in Lord Worplesdon's service for nearly a year, during which time I had ample opportunities of studying her ladyship. The opinion of the servants' hall was far from favourable to her. Her ladyship's temper caused a good deal of adverse comment among us. It was at times quite impossible. You would not have been happy, sir!"

"Get out!"

"I think you would also have found her educational methods a little trying, sir. I have glanced at the book her ladyship gave you – it has been lying on your table since our arrival – and it is, in my opinion, quite unsuitable. You would not have enjoyed it. And I have it from her ladyship's own maid, who happened to overhear a conversation between her ladyship and one of the gentlemen staying here – Mr. Maxwell, who is employed in an editorial capacity by one of the reviews – that it was her intention to start you almost immediately upon Nietzsche. You would not enjoy Nietzsche, sir. He is fundamentally unsound."

"Get out!"

"Very good, sir."

***

It's rummy how sleeping on a thing often makes you feel quite different about it. It's happened to me over and over again. Somehow or other, when I woke next morning the old heart didn't feel half so broken as it had done. It was a perfectly topping day, and there was something about the way the sun came in at the window and the row the birds were kicking up in the ivy that made me half wonder whether Jeeves wasn't right. After all, though she had a wonderful profile, was it such a catch being engaged to Florence Craye as the casual observer might imagine? Wasn't there something in what Jeeves had said about her character? I began to realise that my ideal wife was something quite different, something a lot more clinging and drooping and prattling, and what not.

I had got as far as this in thinking the thing out when that "Types of Ethical Theory" caught my eye. I opened it, and I give you my honest word this was what hit me:

> *Of the two antithetic terms in the Greek philosophy one only was real and self-subsisting; and that one was Ideal Thought as opposed to that which it has to penetrate and*

mould. The other, corresponding to our Nature, was in itself phenomenal, unreal, without any permanent footing, having no predicates that held true for two moments together, in short, redeemed from negation only by including indwelling realities appearing through.

Well – I mean to say – what? And Nietzsche, from all accounts, a lot worse than that!

"Jeeves," I said, when he came in with my morning tea, "I've been thinking it over. You're engaged again."

"Thank you, sir."

I sucked down a cheerful mouthful. A great respect for this bloke's judgment began to soak through me.

"Oh, Jeeves," I said; "about that check suit."

"Yes, sir?"

"Is it really a frost?"

"A trifle too bizarre, sir, in my opinion."

"But lots of fellows have asked me who my tailor is."

"Doubtless in order to avoid him, sir."

"He's supposed to be one of the best men in London."

"I am saying nothing against his moral character, sir."

I hesitated a bit. I had a feeling that I was passing into this chappie's clutches, and that if I gave in now I should become just like poor old Aubrey Fothergill, unable to call my soul my own. On the other hand, this was obviously a cove of rare intelligence, and it would be a comfort in a lot of ways to have him doing the thinking for me. I made up my mind.

"All right, Jeeves," I said. "You know! Give the bally thing away to somebody!"

He looked down at me like a father gazing tenderly at the wayward child.

"Thank you, sir. I gave it to the under-gardener last night. A little more tea, sir?"

DISENTANGLING OLD DUGGIE

Doesn't some poet or philosopher fellow say that it's when our intentions are best that we always make the worst breaks? I can't put my hand on the passage, but you'll find it in Shakespeare or somewhere, I'm pretty certain.

At any rate, it's always that way with me. And the affair of Douglas Craye is a case in point.

I had dined with Duggie (a dear old pal of mine) one night at his club, and as he was seeing me out he said: "Reggie, old top" – my name's Reggie Pepper – "Reggie, old top, I'm rather worried."

"Are you, Duggie, old pal?" I said.

"Yes, Reggie, old fellow," he said, "I am. It's like this. The Booles have asked me down to their place for the week-end, and I don't know whether to go or not. You see, they have early breakfast, and besides that there's a frightful risk of music after dinner. On the other hand, young Roderick Boole thinks he can play piquet."

"I should go," I said.

"But I'm not sure Roderick's going to be there this time."

It was a problem, and I didn't wonder poor old Dug had looked pale and tired at dinner.

Then I had the idea which really started all the trouble.

"Why don't you consult a palmist?" I said.

"That sounds a good idea," said Duggie.

"Go and see Dorothea in Forty-second Street. She's a wonder. She'll settle it for you in a second. She'll see from your lines that you are thinking of making a journey, and she'll either tell you to get a move on, which will mean that Roderick will be there, or else to keep away because she sees disaster."

"You seem to be next to the game all right."

"I've been to a good many of them. You'll like Dorothea."

"What did you say her name was – Dorothea? What do I do? Do I just walk in? Shan't I feel a fearful chump? How much do I give her?"

"Five bucks. You'd better write and make a date."

"All right," said Duggie. "But I know I shall look a frightful fool."

About a week later I ran into him between the acts at the Knickerbocker. The old boy was beaming.

"Reggie," he said, "you did me the best turn anyone's ever done me, sending me to Mrs. Darrell."

"Mrs. Darrell?"

"You know. Dorothea. Her real name's Darrell. She's a widow. Her husband was in some regiment, and left her without a penny. It's a frightfully pathetic story. Haven't time to tell you now. My boy, she's a marvel. She had hardly looked at my hand, when she said: 'You will prosper in any venture you undertake.' And next day, by George,

I went down to the Booles' and separated young Roderick from seventy dollars. She's a wonderful woman. Did you ever see just that shade of hair?"

"I didn't notice her hair."

He gaped at me in a sort of petrified astonishment.

"You – didn't – notice – her – hair!" he gasped.

I can't fix the dates exactly, but it must have been about three weeks after this that I got a telegram:

"Call Madison Avenue immediately–.

"Florence Craye."

She needn't have signed her name. I should have known who it was from by the wording. Ever since I was a kid, Duggie's sister Florence has oppressed me to the most fearful extent. Not that I'm the only one. Her brothers live in terror of her, I know. Especially Edwin. He's never been able to get away from her and it's absolutely broken his spirit. He's a mild, hopeless sort of chump who spends all his time at home – they live near Philadelphia – and has never been known to come to New York. He's writing a history of the family, or something, I believe.

You see, events have conspired, so to speak, to let Florence do pretty much as she likes with them. Originally there was old man Craye, Duggie's father, who made a fortune out of the Soup Trust; Duggie's elder brother Edwin; Florence; and Duggie. Mrs. Craye has been dead some years. Then came the smash. It happened through the old man. Most people, if you ask them, will tell you that he ought to be in Bloomingdale; and I'm not sure they're not right. At any rate, one morning he came down to breakfast, lifted the first cover on the sideboard, said in a sort of despairing way, "Eggs! Eggs! Eggs! Curse all eggs!" and walked out of the room. Nobody thought much of it till about an hour afterward, when they found that he had packed a grip, left the house, and caught the train to New York. Next day they got a letter from him, saying that he was off to Europe, never to return, and that all communications were to be addressed to his lawyers. And from that day on none of them had seen him. He wrote occasionally, generally from Paris; and that was all.

Well, directly news of this got about, down swooped a series of aunts to grab the helm. They didn't stay long. Florence had them out, one after the other, in no time. If any lingering doubt remained in their minds, don't you know, as to who was going to be boss at home, it wasn't her fault. Since then she has run the show.

I went to Madison Avenue. It was one of the aunts' houses. There was no sign of the aunt when I called – she had probably climbed a tree and pulled it up after her – but Florence was there.

She is a tall woman with what, I believe, is called "a presence." Her eyes are bright and black, and have a way of getting right inside you, don't you know, and running up and down your spine. She has a deep voice. She is about ten years older than Duggie's brother Edwin, who is six years older than Duggie.

"Good afternoon," she said. "Sit down."

I poured myself into a chair.

"Reginald," she said, "what is this I hear about Douglas?"

I said I didn't know.

"He says that you introduced him."

"Eh?"

"To this woman – this Mrs. Darrell."

"Mrs. Darrell?"

My memory's pretty rocky, and the name conveyed nothing to me.

She pulled out a letter.

"Yes," she said, "Mrs. Dorothy Darrell."

"Great Scott! Dorothea!"

Her eyes resumed their spine drill.

"Who is she?"

"Only a palmist."

"Only a palmist!" Her voice absolutely boomed. "Well, my brother Douglas is engaged to be married to her."

"Many happy returns of the day," I said.

I don't know why I said it. It wasn't what I meant to say. I'm not sure I meant to say anything.

She glared at me. By this time I was pure jelly. I simply flowed about the chair.

"You are facetious, Reginald," she said.

"No, no, no," I shouted. "It slipped out. I wouldn't be facetious for worlds."

"I am glad. It is no laughing matter. Have you any suggestions?"

"Suggestions?"

"You don't imagine it can be allowed to go on? The engagement must be broken, of course. But how?"

"Why don't you tell him he mustn't?"

"I shall naturally express my strong disapproval, but it may not be effective. When out of the reach of my personal influence, my wretched brother is self-willed to a degree."

I saw what she meant. Good old Duggie wasn't going to have those eyes patrolling his spine if he knew it. He meant to keep away and conduct this business by letter. There was going to be no personal interview with sister, if he had to dodge about America like a snipe.

We sat for a long time without speaking. Then I became rather subtle. I had a brain-wave and saw my way to making things right for Dug and at the same time squaring myself with Florence. After all, I thought, the old boy couldn't keep away from home for the rest of his life. He would have to go there sooner or later. And my scheme made it pleasant and easy for him.

"I'll tell you what I should do if I were you," I said. "I'm not sure I didn't read some book or see some play somewhere or other where they tried it on, and it worked all right. Fellow got engaged to a girl, and the family didn't like it, but, instead of kicking, they pretended to be tickled to pieces, and had the fellow and the girl down to visit them. And then, after the fellow had seen the girl with the home circle as a background, don't you know, he came to the conclusion that it wouldn't do, and broke off the engagement."

It seemed to strike her.

"I hardly expected so sensible a suggestion from you, Reginald," she said. "It is a very good plan. It shows that you really have a definite substratum of intelligence; and it is all the more deplorable that you should idle your way through the world as you do, when you might be performing some really useful work."

That was Florence all over. Even when she patted you on the head, she had to do it with her knuckles.

"I will invite them down next week," she went on. "You had better come, too."

"It's awfully kind of you, but the fact is..."

"Next Wednesday. Take the three-forty-seven."

I met Duggie next day. He was looking happy, but puzzled, like a man who has found a dime on the street and is wondering if there's a string tied to it. I congratulated him on his engagement.

"Reggie," he said, "a queer thing has happened. I feel as if I'd trodden on the last step when it wasn't there. I've just had a letter from my sister Florence asking me to bring Dorothy home on Wednesday. Florence doesn't seem to object to the idea of the engagement at all; and I'd expected that I'd have to call out the police reserves when she heard of it. I believe there's a catch somewhere."

I tapped him on the breastbone.

"There is, Dug," I said, "and I'll tell you what it is. I saw her yesterday, and I can put you next to the game. She thinks that if you see Mrs. Darrell mingling with the home circle, you'll see flaws in her which you don't see when you don't see her mingling with the home circle, don't you see? Do you see now?"

He laughed – heroically, don't you know.

"I'm afraid she'll be disappointed. Love like mine is not dependent on environment."

Which wasn't bad, I thought, if it was his own.

I said good-by to him, and toddled along rather pleased with myself. It seemed to me that I had handled his affairs in a pretty masterly manner for a chap who's supposed to be one of the biggest chumps in New York.

Well, of course, the thing was an absolute fliver, as I ought to have guessed it would be. Whatever could have induced me to think that a fellow like poor old Dug stood a dog's chance against a determined female like his sister Florence, I can't imagine. It was like expecting a rabbit to put up a show with a python. From the very start there was only one possible end to the thing. To a woman like Florence, who had trained herself as tough as whalebone by years of scrapping with her father and occasional by-battles with aunts, it was as easy as killing rats with a stick.

I was sorry for Mrs. Darrell. She was a really good sort and, as a matter of fact, just the kind of wife who would have done old Duggie a bit of good. And on her own ground I shouldn't wonder if she might not have made a fight for it. But now she hadn't a chance. Poor old Duggie was just like so much putty in Florence's hands when he couldn't get away from her. You could see the sawdust trickling out of Love's Young Dream in a steady flow.

I took Mrs. Darrell for a walk one afternoon, to see if I couldn't cheer her up a bit, but it wasn't much good. She hardly spoke a word till we were on our way home. Then she said with a sort of jerk: "I'm going back to New York tomorrow, Mr. Pepper."

I suppose I ought to have pretended to be surprised, but I couldn't work it.

"I'm afraid you've had a bad time," I said. "I'm very sorry."

She laughed.

"Thank you," she said. "It's nice of you to be sympathetic instead of tactful. You're rather a dear, Mr. Pepper."

I hadn't any remarks to make. I whacked at a nettle with my stick.

"I shall break off my engagement after dinner, so that Douglas can have a good night's rest. I'm afraid he has been brooding on the future a good deal. It will be a great relief to him."

"Oh, no," I said.

"Oh, yes. I know exactly how he feels. He thought he could carry me off, but he finds he overestimated his powers. He has remembered that he is a Craye. I imagine that the fact has been pointed out to him."

"If you ask my opinion," I said – I was feeling pretty sore about it – "that woman Florence is an absolute cat."

"My dear Mr. Pepper, I wouldn't have dreamed of asking your opinion on such a delicate subject. But I'm glad to have it. Thank you very much. Do I strike you as a vindictive woman, Mr. Pepper?"

"I don't think you do," I said.

"By nature I don't think I am. But I'm feeling a little vindictive just at present."

She stopped suddenly.

"I don't know why I'm boring you like this, Mr. Pepper," she said. "For goodness' sake let's be cheerful. Say something bright."

I was going to take a whirl at it, but she started in to talk, and talked all the rest of the way. She seemed to have cheered up a whole lot.

She left next day. I gather she fired Duggie as per schedule, for the old boy looked distinctly brighter, and Florence wore an off-duty expression and was quite decently civil. Mrs. Darrell bore up all right. She avoided Duggie, of course, and put in most of the time talking to Edwin. He evidently appreciated it, for I had never seen him look so nearly happy before.

I went back to New York directly afterward, and I hadn't been there much more than a week when a most remarkably queer thing happened. Turning in at Hammerstein's for half an hour one evening, whom should I meet but brother Edwin, quite fairly festive, with a fat cigar in his mouth. "Hello, Reggie," he said.

"What are you doing here?" I said.

"I had to come up to New York to look up a life of Hilary de Craye at the library. I believe Mister Man was a sort of ancestor."

"This isn't the library."

"I was beginning to guess as much. The difference is subtle but well marked."

It struck me that there was another difference that was subtle but well marked, and that was the difference between the Edwin I'd left messing about over his family history a week before and the jovial rounder who was blowing smoke in my face now.

"As a matter of fact," he said, "the library would be all the better for a little of this sort of thing. It's too conservative. That's what's the trouble with the library. What's the matter with having a cross-talk team and a few performing dogs there? It would brighten the place up and attract custom. Reggie, you're looking fatigued. I've heard there's a place somewhere in this city, if you can only find it, expressly designed for supplying first-aid to the fatigued. Let's go and look for it."

I'm not given to thinking much as a rule, but I couldn't help pondering over this meeting with Edwin. It's hard to make you see the remarkableness of the whole thing, for, of course, if you look at it, in one way, there's nothing so record-breaking in smoking a cigar and drinking a high-ball. But then you have never seen Edwin. There are degrees in everything, don't you know. For Edwin to behave as he did with me that night was simply nothing more nor less than a frightful outburst, and it disturbed me. Not that I cared what Edwin did, as a rule, but I couldn't help feeling a sort of what-d'you-call-it – a presentiment, that somehow, in some way I didn't understand, I was mixed up in it, or was soon going to be. I think the whole fearful family had got on my nerves to such an extent that the mere sight of any of them made me jumpy.

And, by George, I was perfectly right, don't you know. In a day or two along came the usual telegram from Florence, telling me to come to Madison Avenue.

The mere idea of Madison Avenue was beginning to give me that tired feeling, and I made up my mind I wouldn't go near the place. But of course I did. When it came to the point, I simply hadn't the common manly courage to keep away.

Florence was there as before.

"Reginald," she said, "I think I shall go raving mad."

This struck me as a mighty happy solution of everybody's troubles, but I felt it was too good to be true.

"Over a week ago," she went on, "my brother Edwin came up to New York to consult a book at the library. I anticipated that this would occupy perhaps an afternoon, and was expecting him back by an early train next day. He did not arrive. He sent an incoherent telegram. But even then I suspected nothing." She paused. "Yesterday morning," she said, "I had a letter from my aunt Augusta."

She paused again. She seemed to think I ought to be impressed.

Her eyes tied a bowknot in my spine.

"Let me read you her letter. No, I will tell you its contents. Aunt Augusta had seen Edwin lunching at the Waldorf with a creature."

"A what?"

"My aunt described her. Her hair was of a curious dull bronze tint."

"Your aunt's?"

"The woman's. It was then that I began to suspect. How many women with dull bronze hair does Edwin know?"

"Great Scott! Why ask me?"

I had got used to being treated as a sort of "Hey, Bill!" by Florence, but I was darned if I was going to be expected to be an encyclopedia as well.

"One," she said. "That appalling Darrell woman."

She drew a deep breath.

"Yesterday evening," she said, "I saw them together in a taximeter cab. They were obviously on their way to some theatre."

She fixed me with her eye.

"Reginald," she said, "you must go and see her the first thing tomorrow."

"What!" I cried. "Me? Why? Why me?"

"Because you are responsible for the whole affair. You introduced Douglas to her. You suggested that he should bring her home. Go to her tomorrow and ascertain her intentions."

"But..."

"The very first thing."

"But wouldn't it be better to have a talk with Edwin?"

"I have made every endeavour to see Edwin, but he deliberately avoids me. His answers to my telegrams are willfully evasive."

There was no doubt that Edwin had effected a thorough bolt. He was having quite a pleasant little vacation: Two Weeks in Sunny New York. And from what I'd seen of him, he seemed to be thriving on it. I didn't wonder Florence had got rather anxious. She'd have been more anxious if she had seen him when I did. He'd got a sort of "New-York-is-so-bracing" look about him, which meant a whole heap of trouble before he trotted back to the fold.

Well, I started off to interview Mrs. Darrell, and, believe me, I didn't like the prospect. I think they ought to train A.D.T. messengers to do this sort of thing. I found her alone. The rush hour of clients hadn't begun.

"How do you do, Mr. Pepper?" she said. "How nice of you to call."

Very friendly, and all that. It made the situation darned difficult for a fellow, if you see what I mean.

"Say," I said. "What about it, don't you know?"

"I certainly don't," she said. "What ought I to know about what?"

"Well, about Edwin – Edwin Craye," I said.

She smiled.

"Oh! So you're an ambassador, Mr. Pepper?"

"Well, as a matter of fact, I did come to see if I could find out how things were running. What's going to happen?"

"Are you consulting me professionally? If so, you must show me your hand. Or perhaps you would rather I showed you mine?"

It was subtle, but I got on to it after a bit.

"Yes," I said, "I wish you would."

"Very well. Do you remember a conversation we had, Mr. Pepper, my last afternoon at the Crayes'? We came to the conclusion that I was rather a vindictive woman."

"By George! You're stringing old Edwin so as to put one over on Florence?"

She flushed a little.

"How very direct you are, Mr. Pepper! How do you know I'm not very fond of Mr. Craye? At any rate, I'm very sorry for him."

"He's such a chump."

"But he's improving every day. Have you seen him? You must notice the difference?"

"There is a difference."

"He only wanted taking out of himself. I think he found his sister Florence's influence a little oppressive sometimes."

"No, but see here," I said, "are you going to marry him?"

"I'm only a palmist. I don't pretend to be a clair-voyant. A marriage may be indicated in Mr. Craye's hand, but I couldn't say without looking at it."

"But I shall have to tell her something definite, or she won't give me a moment's peace."

"Tell her her brother is of age. Surely that's definite enough?"

And I couldn't get any more out of her. I went back to Florence and reported. She got pretty excited about it.

"Oh, if I were a man!" she said.

I didn't see how that would have helped. I said so.

"I'd go straight to Edwin and *drag* him away. He is staying at his club. If I were a man I could go in and find him..."

"Not if you weren't a member," I said.

"–And tell him what I thought of his conduct. As I'm only a woman, I have to wait in the hall while a deceitful small boy pretends to go and look for him."

It had never struck me before what a splendid institution a club was. Only a few days back I'd been thinking that the subscription to mine was a bit steep. But now I saw that the place earned every cent of the money.

"Have you no influence with him, Reginald?"

I said I didn't think I had. She called me something. Invertebrate, or something. I didn't catch it.

"Then there's only one thing to do. You must find my father and tell him all. Perhaps you may rouse him to a sense of what is right. You may make him remember that he has duties as a parent."

I thought it far more likely that I should make him remember that he had a foot. I hadn't a very vivid recollection of old man Craye. I was quite a kid when he made his great speech on the Egg Question and beat it for Europe – but what I did recollect didn't encourage me to go and chat with him about the duties of a parent.

As I remember him, he was a rather large man with elephantiasis of the temper. I distinctly recalled one occasion when I was spending a school vacation at his home, and he found me trying to shave old Duggie, then a kid of fourteen, with his razor.

"I shouldn't be able to find him," I said.

"You can get his address from his lawyers."

"He may be at the North Pole."

"Then you must go to the North Pole."

"But say–!"

"Reginald!"

"Oh, all right."

I knew just what would happen. Parbury and Stevens, the lawyers, simply looked at me as if I had been caught snatching bags. At least, Stevens did. And Parbury would have done it, too, only he had been dead a good time. Finally, after drinking me in for about a quarter of an hour, Stevens said that if I desired to address a communication to his client, care of this office, it would be duly forwarded. Good morning. Good morning. Anything further? No, thanks. Good morning. Good morning.

I handed the glad news on to Florence and left her to do what she liked about it. She went down and interviewed Stevens. I suppose he'd had experience of her. At any rate, he didn't argue. He yielded up the address in level time. Old man Craye was living in Paris, but was to arrive in New York that night, and would doubtless be at his club.

It was the same club where Edwin was hiding from Florence. I pointed this out to her.

"There's no need for me to butt in after all," I said. "He'll meet Edwin there, and they can fight it out in the smoking room. You've only to drop him a line explaining the facts."

"I shall certainly communicate with him in writing, but, nevertheless, you must see him. I cannot explain everything in a letter."

"But doesn't it strike you that he may think it pretty bad gall-impertinence, don't you know, for a comparative stranger like me to be tackling a delicate family affair like this?"

"You will explain that you are acting for me."

"It wouldn't be better if old Duggie went along instead?"

"I wish you to go, Reginald."

Well, of course, it was all right, don't you know, but I was losing several pounds a day over the business. I was getting so light that I felt that, when the old man kicked me, I should just soar up to the ceiling like an air balloon.

The club was one of those large clubs that look like prisons. I used to go there to lunch with my uncle, the one who left me his money, and I always hated the place. It was one of those clubs that are all red leather and hushed whispers.

I'm bound to say, though, there wasn't much hushed whispering when I started my interview with old man Craye. His voice was one of my childhood's recollections.

He was most extraordinarily like Florence. He had just the same eyes. I felt boneless from the start.

"Good morning," I said.

"What?" he said. "Speak up. Don't mumble."

I hadn't known he was deaf. The last time we'd had any conversation – on the subject of razors – he had done all the talking. This seemed to me to put the lid on it.

"I only said 'Good morning,'" I shouted.

"Good what? Speak up. I believe you're sucking candy. Oh, good morning? I remember you now. You're the boy who spoiled my razor."

I didn't half like this reopening of old wounds. I hurried on.

"I came about Edwin," I said.

"Who?"

"Edwin. Your son."

"What about him?"

"Florence told me to see you."

"Who?"

"Florence. Your daughter."

"What about her?"

All this vaudeville team business, mind you, as if we were bellowing at each other across the street. All round the room you could see old gentlemen shooting out of their chairs like rockets and dashing off at a gallop to write to the governing board about it. Thousands of waiters had appeared from nowhere, and were hanging about, dusting table legs. If ever a business wanted to be discussed privately, this seemed to me to be it. And it was just about as private as a conversation through megaphones in Longacre Square.

"Didn't she write to you?"

"I got a letter from her. I tore it up. I didn't read it."

Pleasant, was it not? It was not. I began to understand what a shipwrecked sailor must feel when he finds there's something gone wrong with the life belt.

I thought I might as well get to the point and get it over.

"Edwin's going to marry a palmist," I said.

"Who the devil's Harry?"

"Not Harry. Marry. He's going to marry a palmist."

About four hundred waiters noticed a speck of dust on an ash tray at the table next to ours, and swooped down on it.

"Edwin is going to marry a palmist?"

"Yes."

"She must be mad. Hasn't she seen Edwin?"

And just then who should stroll in but Edwin himself. I sighted him and gave him a hail.

He curveted up to us. It was amazing the way the fellow had altered. He looked like a two-year-old. Flower in his button-hole and a six-inch grin, and all that. The old man seemed surprised, too. I didn't wonder. The Edwin he remembered was a pretty different kind of a fellow.

"Hullo, dad," he said. "Fancy meeting you here. Have a cigarette?"

He shoved out his case. Old man Craye helped himself in a sort of dazed way.

"You *are* Edwin?" he said slowly.

I began to sidle out. They didn't notice me. They had moved to a settee, and Edwin seemed to be telling his father a funny story.

At least, he was talking and grinning, and the old man was making a noise like distant thunder, which I supposed was his way of chuckling. I slid out and left them.

Some days later Duggie called on me. The old boy was looking scared.

"Reggie," he said, "what do doctors call it when you think you see things when you don't? Hal-something. I've got it, whatever it is. It's sometimes caused by overwork. But it can't be that with me, because I've not been doing any work. You don't think my brain's going or anything like that, do you?"

"What do you mean? What's been happening?"

"It's like being haunted. I read a story somewhere of a fellow who kept thinking he saw a battleship bearing down on him. I've got it, too. Four times in the last three days I could have sworn I saw my father and Edwin. I saw them as plainly as I see you. And, of course, Edwin's at home and father's in Europe somewhere. Do you think it's some sort of a warning? Do you think I'm going to die?"

"It's all right, old top," I said. "As a matter of fact, they are both in New York just now."

"You don't mean that? Great Scot, what a relief! But, Reggie, old fox, it couldn't have been them really. The last time was at Louis Martin's, and the fellow I mistook for Edwin was dancing all by himself in the middle of the floor."

I admitted it was pretty queer.

I was away for a few days after that in the country. When I got back I found a pile of telegrams waiting for me. They were all from Florence, and they all wanted me to go to Madison Avenue. The last of the batch, which had arrived that morning, was so peremptory that I felt as if something had bitten me when I read it.

For a moment I admit I hung back. Then I rallied. There are times in a man's life when he has got to show a flash of the old bulldog pluck, don't you know, if he wants to preserve his self-respect. I did then. My grip was still unpacked. I told my man to put it on a cab. And in about two ticks I was bowling off to the club. I left for England next day by the *Lusitania*.

About three weeks later I fetched up at Nice. You can't walk far at Nice without bumping into a casino. The one I hit my first evening was the Casino Municipale in the Place Masséna. It looked more or less of a Home From Home, so I strolled in.

There was quite a crowd round the boule tables, and I squashed in. And when I'd worked through into the front rank I happened to look down the table, and there was Edwin, with a green Tyrolese hat hanging over one ear, clutching out for a lot of five-franc pieces which the croupier was steering toward him at the end of a rake.

I was feeling lonesome, for I knew no one in the place, so I edged round in his direction.

Halfway there I heard my name called, and there was Mrs. Darrell.

I saw the whole thing in a flash. Old man Craye hadn't done a thing to prevent it – apart from being eccentric, he was probably glad that Edwin had had the sense to pick out anybody half as good a sort – and the marriage had taken place. And here they were on their honeymoon.

I wondered what Florence was thinking of it.

"Well, well, well, here we all are," I said. "I've just seen Edwin. He seems to be winning."

"Dear boy!" she said. "He does enjoy it so. I think he gets so much more out of life than he used to, don't you?"

"Sure thing. May I wish you happiness? Why didn't you let me know and collect the silver fish-slice?"

"Thank you so much, Mr. Pepper. I did write to you, but I suppose you never got the letter."

"Mr. Craye didn't make any objections, then?"

"On the contrary. He was more in favor of the marriage than anyone."

"And I'll tell you why," I said. "I'm rather a chump, you know, but I observe things. I bet he was most frightfully grateful to you for taking Edwin in hand and making him human."

"Why, you're wonderful, Mr. Pepper. That is exactly what he said himself. It was that that first made us friends."

"And – er – Florence?"

She sighed.

"I'm afraid Florence has taken the thing a little badly. But I hope to win her over in time. I want all my children to love me."

"All your what?"

"I think of them as my children, you see, Mr. Pepper. I adopted them as my own when I married their father. Did you think I had married Edwin? What a funny mistake. I am very fond of Edwin, but not in that way. No, I married Mr. Craye. We left him at our villa tonight, as he had some letters to get off. You must come and see us, Mr. Pepper. I always feel that it was you who brought us together, you know. I wonder if you will be seeing Florence when you get back? Will you give her my very best love?"

Books For ALL Kinds of Readers

At ReadHowYouWant we understand that one size does not fit all types of readers. Our innovative, patent pending technology allows us to design new formats to make reading easier and more enjoyable for you. This helps improve your speed of reading and your comprehension. Our EasyRead printed books have been optimized to improve word recognition, ease eye tracking by adjusting word and line spacing as well as minimizing hyphenation. Our EasyRead SuperLarge editions have been developed to make reading easier and more accessible for vision-impaired readers. We offer Braille and DAISY formats of our books and all popular E-Book formats.

Printed in Great Britain
by Amazon

42389884R00120